About the author

Ajay K Pandey grew up in the modest NTPC township of Rihand Nagar with big dreams. He studied Engineering in Electronics at IERT (Allahabad) and MBA at IIMM (Pune) before taking up a job in a corporate firm.

He grew up with a dream of becoming a teacher, but destiny landed him in the IT field. Travelling, trekking and reading novels are his hobbies. Travelling to different places has taught him about different cultures and people, and makes him wonder how despite all the differences, there is a bond that unites them. Trekking always inspires him to deal with challenges like a sport. Reading is perhaps what makes him feel alive.

You Are the Best Wife is his debut book based on his life events and lessons. Apart from writing, he wants to follow his role model Mother Teresa and create a charitable trust to support aged people and educate special children.

After his debut book *You Are the Best Wife*, Ajay has authored bestselling titles *Her Last Wish, You Are the Best Friend, An Unexpected Gift, A Girl to Remember* and *Everything I Never Told You*.

Ajay is more active on Instagram and Twitter, and you can reach him at:

Facebook: *AuthorAjayPandey*
Twitter: *@AjayPandey_08*
Instagram: *@author_ajaykpandey*
Email: *ajaypandey0807@gmail.com*

By the same author

Praise for the author and his works:

"Can an IT professional write bestselling books? Ajay Pandey, the author of two bestsellers would have an answer to this."

—*The Hindu*

"Bhavna's last words become strength for Ajay, who lives to fulfil his promise of love."

—*Business Standard*

"... channelise his agony into writing. The result? Two best-selling novels, You Are the Best Wife and Her Last Wish, based on a true love story.

—*The Asian Age*

"... a semi-autobiographical book on vanquishing loneliness."

—*Mid-Day*

"... anyone who is going through a rough phase in terms of a personal relationship must read this."

—*Deccan Chronicle*

"...beat the likes of JK Rowling and Devdutt Pattanaik to go to the top of the bestselling list in India."

—*Mid-Day*

"...Ajay K Pandey hit the big league of pulpy romance"

—*Quartz India*

"... a bestselling book is made."

—*Scroll.in*

"The real love story will pull you in a pool of emotions."

—*Jagran*

"There are some books that are not just stories but reflection of realities of life. You are the Best Wife is one such book.

—*WritersMelon*

"The Indian author has given reasons to believe that India has not only given good tech-heads, but are delivering literary moths too."

—*The Truth India*

"...sold over a lakh copies... connected with the masses in a way no previous author has ever done."

—*BookGeeks.in*

"The loving heart of a beautiful soul Bhavna, encouraged Ajay to fight back and start looking at life in a positive way."

—*India Café 24*

"It is one of the purest, heart-warming love stories I ever read..."

—*Salisonline.in*

The Girl in the Red Lipstick

AJAY K PANDEY

Srishti
Publishers & Distributors

Srishti Publishers & Distributors
A unit of AJR Publishing LLP
212A, Peacock Lane
Shahpur Jat, New Delhi – 110 049
editorial@srishtipublishers.com

First published by
Srishti Publishers & Distributors in 2021

10 9 8 7 6 5 4 3

This is a work of fiction. The characters, places, organizations and events described in this book are either a work of the author's imagination or have been used fictitiously. Any resemblance to people, living or dead, places, events, communities or organizations is purely coincidental.

Printed and bound in India

Dedicated to
the girl I met in Kolkata.

Always call a prostitute a lady; you have no idea what she has been through.

–Arun Kumar

A note from the author

Hi friends,

The idea of writing this book sprouted when I met a strange girl in the sparkling Park Street in Kolkata. Although the story has some slices of my life, I have fictionalised several bits. Which parts are true and which parts are fictional, that I would leave to your judgment.

This book is a small attempt to offer respect to the struggling red-light area girls. I wish I could do something more than merely writing a book.

My respect to my entire family, that stood by me and decided to take each step with me.

Heartfelt gratitude to the exceptional team at Srishti Publishers for their superb guidance. A special mention to Jayanta Bose, Arup Bose and Stuti.

Love and thanks to Merril Anil for her contribution to the book.

Many thanks to my friends from the film world – Adit Singh and Mahesh Balraj.

Thank you, Satish and Gautam sir for showing your faith in me.

A big thank you to my readers for accepting my crazy stories. I am more active on Instagram (@author_ajaykpandey) and Twitter. Please do connect. I try hard to reply to each and every message and comment that I get there. Believe it or not, it is you who have made me what I am today.

I take this opportunity to thank all the wonderful hearts who supported me in their own individual way. Your reviews and feedback are the silent, but efficient way, to enrich an author.

Thank you for making me an author, though I would always politely ask you to treat me as your "author friend".

Never surrender!

Ajay

1

The quick Kolkata trip

I landed at the Kolkata airport with a small handbag for my two-day trip. I rubbed my eyes and opened them slowly. I had slept through the early morning flight from Pune. I walked out of the exit gate, straight into a crowd staring yearningly at every passenger that walked out, flashing the placards they were holding. I scanned the platter of names spread for one's picking. There were the mundane Mr Dutta, Mrs Mukherjee and Dr Dhillon, among a few high-end surnames like Mr Jindal, Mr Kapoor and Mr Bhatt.

I glanced at this sea of names and finally spotted mine, held by a man dressed in an old-fashioned white chauffeur's uniform. I tilted my neck a little. He must have guessed from my body language that I was his pick for the day. I read the name on the placard – "Arun Kumar".

He approached me with a smile and I took in more of his appearance. Slightly dark complexioned, he was totally soaked in white, including the shining teeth that perfectly matched his attire. It was a vision to behold. While I was busy analysing his appearance, he had already taken the handbag from me and walked towards his car. He stood next to it, waiting.

'Saab, Hotel Peerless?'

'Yes. Do you know where it is?'

He nodded in response and flashed me a smile. I walked towards the front door and saw through the window that the seat had newspapers, a charger and water bottles on it.

'Will you be sitting in the front, saab?' he asked, somewhat staggered at my approach.

'Yes.'

He rushed to clear the front seat, throwing stuff haphazardly on the back seat.

'Do you want me to sit at the back?' I asked, feeling as if I had broken some unsaid protocol of sitting in a cab.

'No sir! Please sit wherever you want,' he said, flashing his teeth.

'What is your name?' I asked him after I had settled down in the front seat.

'It's Rakesh, sir.'

'Nice name.'

'Sir, are you coming here for the first time?' He put the car into first gear and we started towards our destination.

'No, no. This is my fourth visit.'

'Oh, nice! So what is your plan for the next two days?'

'Will you be with me for the entire trip?'

'Yes, sir. The company has instructed me to be with you for two days.'

'Well, in that case, I have a session at Prince College around 2 p.m. today.'

'Oh, are you a teacher?'

'No, I am an author. The college has called me for a guest lecture, and I will also be launching my book tomorrow at South Avenue mall at 4 p.m.'

'Ok sir,' he said with a huge smile. Oddly enough, it gave me a feeling that I had passed some kind of a screening test with him. I yawned and rubbed my eyes. He glanced at me twice, and I understood that he wanted to ask more.

'What kind of books do you write, sir?'

'Mostly love stories. Do you read love stories?'

'Yes, I have read a lot of *prem kahani*. Love stories, I mean.'

'That's great!' For the first time since we had met, I returned his smile. It wasn't, of course, with the same intensity as his.

I was about to ask him if he also read books in English, but I avoided saying it out loud. It didn't seem right to ask that. We live in a country where English is not a language, but a status symbol.

'Sir, my brother-in-law is also an author,' he said, beaming with pride. 'He has written so many stories.'

I narrowed my eyes and tried to read him. 'Really?'

In my observation, every time I mentioned I had written books, people usually responded that some of their far or close relative was an upcoming author. But this time, coming from a taxi driver, it was a little unusual.

'What kind of stories?'

'All his stories are about love, and only love.' The vanity on his face was reflected in his sparkling eyes.

'Okay! Why don't you tell me some of the names!' I instantly pulled my mobile phone out, ready to search for the books on the web.

'I have not read many of them.' He blushed a little.

'Not even one?' I raised my eyebrows and shrugged my shoulders.

'No no! I have read a few. I think the first was *Bengal ki Rani* or Queen of Bengal, and the second was *Kaatil Jawani*. I lost track of the names after these two.'

'Hmm, these are love stories?'

'Pure love!'

'Okay! What were those stories about?'

'Not story, sir. Only love.'

'Not a story?' I rubbed my forehead. 'What does that mean?' My curiosity was swiftly metamorphosing into confusion, and giving me a headache.

'Only love-making, sir ji! And it had a lot of pictures too.' He blushed and I understood what this rarest of rare new genre was all about, which came with no story, but just love-making.

'You mean adult books?' I asked.

'Yes. We normally call them *mastram*, not adult love stories.'

'Oh!' I groaned. The conversation was now becoming cringe-worthy. I made a mental note of how a few people still did not know the difference between love and sex.

'Sir, do you need a copy?'

'No! I prefer a love story. If there is no story, then there is no love as well.'

After an hour of braving through the traffic, we reached Hotel Peerless. I noticed from the parking area how ordinary the hotel looked from outside even now. Well, the owner was a great fan of surprise element. In extreme contrast to its dull white exterior, the hotel resembled a mini palace from inside. The massive lobby was a magnificent vision in gold and ivory, sparkling with a glimmer from all corners. The aesthetic stairs that took its visitors to the rooms radiated the royal aura of the place. The first time I had visited Kolkata, I stayed at this hotel. Ever since, it had became my go-to place in Kolkata.

I checked-in and settled in my comfortable room. The best part about the room was the balcony and the spectacular view it offered. I went to the balcony and lit a cigarette, trying to soak in the mesmerising skyline.

After a relaxing shower and lunch, I brushed through my thoughts for my lecture on "How modern love is distracting youth from studies".

I repeated the title out loud, twice. It felt like a moral science lecture and I was trying to think of some interesting angle to it. I picked up my phone and checked Instagram. It flashed 232 notifications, 44 new followers and 15 pending good morning messages. And that was quite usual for me, as I already had close to 88,000 followers. With 44 new followers in 4 hours, I started calculating mentally, how long it would take to reach the one lakh milestone.

I switched on the video recorder and started recording a video. I was hoping my smile would hush up any residue of a rushed morning.

'Hello, Kolkata friends and students! I will be in Prince College tomorrow, for a session on how modern love is distracting the youth. I am thrilled to see you.'

I scrutinized the recorded video and found that while pronouncing the word 'thrilled', the thrill was clearly missing from my face. I re-recorded and found that I was smiling too much, and then in the third attempt, I found a fault with my pronunciation. After that, I lost count of the retakes. I found ten recorded videos sitting in my gallery, taking space, but none good enough. So after the eleventh take, I stopped focusing on all those aspects and posted it on Instagram directly.

Next morning, I was finishing my breakfast when I received a call.

'Good morning, sir,' echoed a sweet voice. 'This is Sujata from Prince College. I am coordinating today's event, sir. I was wondering when you will be reaching the college.'

'Hi Sujata, I will be there in the next forty-five minutes or so,' I replied, simultaneously gathering my stuff and getting ready to head out.

I stepped out of the hotel after a bit and found Rakesh, the chauffeur, waiting for me. I decided to take the back seat this time. After crossing five turns and two tram lanes, brushing past uncountable vehicles, we finally reached the college. I had informed Sujata that I was on my way and by the time I reached the college premises, she was already waiting for me at the entry gate.

She escorted me to the principal's office, and quite unlike me, I didn't notice much of what was happening around me. My mind was in overdrive, mentally prepping for my session.

'Hope you had a pleasant stay,' the principal asked after offering the usual pleasantries.

I could sense it was an indirect way to emphasise that they were paying for my opulent accommodation.

'It is really good, thank you,' I said with a smile.

After a brief conversation, she directed me towards the auditorium. It was quite spacious and well-planned, I noticed. My guess was that it could easily accommodate around five hundred people. Fortunately, the hall was just half full, yet, and I could see more girls than boys in the audience. Sujata guided me to a seat right next to the principal. I had just settled into the plush seat when I noticed the stage backdrop. I had never seen such a life-size image of myself, almost gigantic. My face and my smile looked endearing in the picture, making me ponder over the last time I had smiled like that! No points for guessing it was one of my favourite pictures, which I usually shared for public printing and displays.

My chain of thoughts was broken with a student taking charge of the microphone. She introduced herself as Pallavi and started reading from her prepared notes.

'Today, we have a special guest with us. He doesn't need any introduction. Arun Kumar sir has authored ten books that have made new records each time, but is still best known for his first book. He left his work in an IT company and finally decided to follow his passion for writing. Apart from writing, he wishes to follow his role model Mother Teresa and give back to the society. He aspires to start a charitable trust that supports the aged and facilitates education for children with special needs.'

I gulped down the appreciation as I processed the long speech, amazed at how she had started with 'he doesn't need an introduction' in the first place. It was still a puzzle for me – how I managed to take the leap by leaving the corporate job amidst all those difficulties, eventually landing in the writing field.

Two beautiful ladies, donning traditional Bengali sarees and wearing red bindis on their forehead neared me. I took in a deep breath and behaved as if everything was normal around me. One of them almost whispered that I should take the stage, just as the other gestured with her hands towards the dais.

'Sir, we welcome you on stage,' Pallavi spoke a little too loudly, perhaps to grab my attention, which was clearly somewhere else.

'Oh yes!' The long introduction must have taken me to a reverie. I got up from my seat and took the mic.

From where I stood, I could see more than two hundred students clapping. It was not the first time that I was seeing or speaking to such a large gathering, but nonetheless, I got carried away with the love and affection showered on me. Every single time. I wished my father could see this.

'Thank you for such a warm welcome.'

Before I could start sharing with these students the depth of my knowledge, one of the girls who had earlier guided me to the stage placed a paper in front me. It had something scribbled in neat handwriting:

Sir, there is an after-lunch session. If possible, please try to wrap up the points in twenty minutes and we can have a longer Q-A session.

I looked back at the audience and noticed a few attendees, including the principal, trying to stifle their yawns. There was absolute silence. I couldn't decide if twenty minutes was also short enough time, or would that put a few to sleep.

There was a huge halogen light directly above my head, which made it tough for me to see faces of the audience clearly. I requested Pallavi to have the lights switched off, but in response, I got a fresh note:

Sir, they will start to fall asleep if we switch the light off.

Fair point! I could endure the piercing light for a bit, because the front row people were clearly drowsy. Quite mechanically, I started delivering my speech, and almost after thirteen minutes, I took a pause to gauge the audience. Before I could resume, a few had started clapping and everyone followed. I understood that they wouldn't be able to bear with me beyond that. I flushed and ended the speech with a short message.

The anchor literally pounced on the mic and announced, 'The floor is open for your questions for half an hour.'

I gulped my saliva like it was mango pulp. How could anyone ask a question when they hadn't even heard me!

'Who wants to go first?' Pallavi said excitedly, not in the least bothered about the worries clawing my mind.

One hand came up and I thanked my stars. At least someone was awake!

'Sir, why do you always write about sex with a female?' she asked in Bengali-soaked English. I frowned, rubbing my chin.

'Could you please specify which book you are talking about?'

There was absolute silence in the auditorium. From the question, I understood that she had not read my works at all. I was put off, but clenched my fingers into a fist and closed my eyes for a second before asking, 'In which book have I mentioned sex with a woman?'

'In all your books.'

'There is no sex scene in any of my books,' I said, loud and clear.

'*Best Wife, Best girl, A Beautiful Girl...* Why do you write only about females?' This time, she asked in Hindi with a predominant Bengali accent.

'Oh!' And then it dawned. 'You meant, why do I only write about women? Is that the question?'

'Yes.'

There was laughter in the hall, which was such a welcome relief. It also showed that the audience was still alive.

'I write mostly about women because I respect them.'

No sooner had I finished my answer that five students raised their hand. Luckily, the questions were the standard ones and went on to create a safe and enjoyable session. After a couple of more usual questions, one rather interesting question was raised. I wasn't expecting it, and it sent me into a tizzy.

'Why haven't you ever written about a prostitute?'

I gulped my hesitation; I did not have a ready answer. There was an awkward silence in the auditorium, but Pallavi came to my rescue and took charge.

'Folks, thank you for the wonderful session. We will close it here. Thank you, Arun sir.'

I thanked her for rescuing me and started moving towards the exit. My mind was abuzz with thoughts about the last question. I climbed down the stairs and missed some steps, collapsing on the floor.

2

I was drowning in an ocean of pain, the fall had been so terrible. By the time I came to my senses, I was being lifted by a few male students. The excruciating pain ran through my back like fire. I must have tumbled at a very bad angle; my neck was twisted slightly towards the left side. Leave aside my attempt to lift my shoulder, it was hard to even move. I wondered how I had ended up falling off this severely.

The students asked me if I was okay, or if I needed any medical assistance. But I wanted to get back to the hotel and lie down. They assisted me till the cab and Rakesh further lent a hand to help me settle inside the car.

When we had driven for a while, Rakesh asked me, having no clue as to what my body was going through, 'What is the plan for tomorrow, sir?'

'We will start from the hotel at around 3.30 p.m. tomorrow.' I groaned in pain.

'When are you going back?'

'Day after tomorrow. I have an early morning flight to Pune.'

It was clearly the most excruciating journey of my life. With every turn and speed breaker, the pain kept worsening. I was driven to the verge of screaming. I knew my body would need a lot of time to heal now.

'Could you please help me to my room?' I had almost run out of breath. I requested Rakesh once we reached the hotel.

'Sure, sir,' he promptly agreed and came to my side to open the car door for me.

He offered his shoulder to support me and wrapped my weak arm around his neck. We entered the hotel lobby and I noticed the hotel staff staring at me. I scanned a few faces; all of them reflected sympathy for me.

Rakesh helped me to my room and lowered me towards the bed. I fell on it like a corpse.

'Sir, may I know where exactly do you have pain?'

He touched my back and when he reached somewhere in the middle, I screamed.

'*Bujhe chhi...*' He responded all-knowingly to my painful screams. 'Sir, you need a deep massage,' he almost declared.

'And how do *you* know that?'

'My jijaji had the same problem.'

I flushed. Honestly, I wanted to kill him. I had no energy or inclination left to have a mindless discussion with him. I closed my eyes and pretended to be tired, all set to sleep. Rakesh took the cue, fortunately, and left me to my misery.

In feigning fatigue, I ended up falling asleep in real. I must have slept for a long time because by the time I woke up, it was dark outside. When I tried moving, I felt slightly relieved from the pain. I picked up the phone and ordered a coffee. I sat up and waited to see how my back was feeling. It was hard to bend my back. I decided to take some medicine for it because I didn't want to extend my stay in Kolkata at any cost. That is when I remembered Fawaz. He worked as a relationship manager in this hotel and had been of help on earlier occasions too.

I dialled his number.

'Hey, Mr Fawaz! This is Arun Kumar. I am at the hotel right now and need some help.'

'Of course, sir. Tell me the room number. I will be there in a sec.'

It was in Fawaz's nature to make the guests feel like celebrities. Naturally, that made him quite popular and one of the reasons why one preferred this hotel over others. With me also, he always behaved like a buddy, as if he knew me since childhood. This time around too, he came into my room using the master key.

After the usual pleasantries, I explained to him what had happened and the pain I was in.

'Sorry to see you in this condition, sir. Where exactly are you feeling the pain?'

He started pressing my back gently and I almost laughed at the realization that everyone becomes a doctor in India if you are in pain.

As he reached the centre of pain, I once again screamed, 'Here, here!'

'I can call a doctor for you,' Fawaz offered, withdrawing his hand quickly.

'Sure. Do you have someone in the hotel? And how much will it cost?'

'No, someone reliable from close by. He would charge about three thousand rupees. If they need to do X-ray or MRI, then that would be extra.'

Only three thousand rupees? Was he crazy! Just hearing the amount was enough for me to decide that I would rather lie on the bed like a corpse, screaming in pain. The financial blow was much worse than the back pain.

He was a smart relationship manager and understood my silence. He suggested, 'Sir, a massage might help.'

'Really?' He was the second person to advise that.

'We have a spa in our hotel that you can try.'

'Can someone come to my room for the massage?'

'It's on the same floor, sir, so should not be a problem for you.'

I nodded thoughtfully and decided to visit the spa after Fawaz left.

The spa was literally next door, but with the pain and lack of support, I felt as if I had walked to the other end of the city to reach the spa. A huge black statue of Buddha in meditation greeted me at the entrance. I saw a young lady dressed in a green uniform at the welcome desk inside. She seemed engrossed in some magazine. I noticed how the spa interiors had an aesthetically calming feel to it. The fresh floral arrangements and fragrance from the incense diffuser led to instant relaxation.

The shiny wooden floor and small tea lights on the desk were giving a heavenly feeling. The walls and ceiling were covered in a thick wall paper with green leaves all over it.

'How can I help you, sir?' the lady asked as soon as she noticed me.

'I suffered a fall and have a severe pain in the lower back. I need a massage for that.'

'Sure sir. Here is our service catalogue.' She handed me a card filled with all kinds of fancy names, but what caught my attention were the extra zeroes against each service. Swedish massage 3000, body massage 3000, oil massage 4000. The zeroes started increasing exponentially as I started going further down the list. I realized the importance of zeroes in life. Also, the pain in my heart was more than the pain in the back.

'Sir, which service would you like to avail?' She flashed an ear-to-ear fake smile. Clearly, she was not impressed with the time I was taking.

I shook my head in the negative.

Fathoming my internal conflict of whether to go for the spa or not, she added, 'For valued customers of the hotel, there is a special discount. It is usually for 4000, but after discount, you will have to pay only 3000.'

I took a deep breath. Her benevolence was too much, but she was dealing with an author, not a businessman.

'You can even choose who you want the session from,' she said pushing an album towards me.

My eyes sparkled when I held the album. The first reaction was 'Wow!' All the girls were rather pretty, as if silently urging me to use their services. I skimmed through the pages and understood why the massage was so costly.

She stretched her hand and flipped open the last page. A beautiful woman was smiling in a small poppy dress. The girl behind the counter flashed a fake smile, adding, 'She is very good at massages.'

I scanned the image again and felt I had seen her somewhere. I gazed the receptionist and she blushed a little. 'Sir, it's me.'

I looked at her face and the picture again. 'Really?'

'Yes sir,' she said biting her lower lip.

I understood she could easily burn a big hole in my cashless pocket.

I handed her the album and returned to my room. Before I could settle down, there was a knock at the door.

It was Fawaz. 'Sir, you did not avail the spa services?'

'Actually...' I struggled to find the right words, not knowing how to convey my financial restrictions to him.

'It was costly *kya*?' I did not deny. 'I can call someone from outside for a massage too.'

'How much do they charge for that?'

'It'll be 1200 for an hour-long massage, and the rest depends on the services you further wish to avail.'

'Hmm, that's nice. The hotel spa is a rip-off.'

I thought for a few seconds and confirmed, 'Okay, you can call someone. But please make sure they are experienced and good. I don't want to break my back completely. I hope you understand.'

'Yes.'

He stood at the corner of the room and his body language conveyed that he needed the cash upfront. So I paid him the entire amount.

He kept two-hundred rupees in his pocket and gave the thousand rupees back.

'You can give the rest of the amount to the massage girl yourself. The rest is between you and her. He flashed a smile and I understood that he had minted two hundred rupees from me even in such a painful condition.

3

When the doorbell rang almost an hour later, I was somewhere in between sleep and restlessness. There was a knock on the door, followed by the bell again. I tried to lift my neck a little and landed back on the bed. My pain-soaked body refused to get up. I rolled a little and summoned all my courage to walk towards the door. I was greeted by a young girl who was wearing a broad smile and rather short clothes. She simply walked into the room, without waiting for my permission.

I took a long look at the lady who had walked into *my* room as if *she* owned it. I guessed she'd be in her early twenties. The blood-red lipstick and the dark kajal applied so lavishly made her look older than she was. The lipstick colour matched perfectly with the dress clinging to her curves, settled far above her knees, as if defying gravity. She had thrown a pink scarf around her neck to give it a chic look.

As soon as she settled on the couch, she removed her scarf. The dangerously low neckline gave an abundant preview of her milky-white complexion. I forgot why she was here until Fawaz entered the room with a ridiculous smile.

'How are you doing, sir?'

'Is she here for the massage?'

He nodded and left the room without another word, closing the door after him. I could only stare at the closed door for a while.

'Sir, I am Lalita.' She extended her hand for a handshake.

'I am Arun,' I mumbled in response.

'So, how do you want to go about this?' I asked as I slowly walked towards my bed.

'With the body...' she said with a wicked grin. An unknown sensation ran through me. My breath became heavy.

'But where are the oils?' I asked after noticing that she only had a tiny purse with her

'You need an oil massage or balm?'

'Balm would be nice.' Anything to relieve the godforsaken back-pain, I thought.

'I will give you whatever you want,' she said and bit her red lips.

I did not reply to her expression. I had failed to appreciate anything about her. I just laid down and signalled that I was ready for the massage. I saw her sitting on the sofa like an esteemed guest.

'Can we start the action?'

'Sure.' I hated the lack of civility I had exhibited to her till now, mostly because of the pain I was in. 'Make yourself comfortable. Do you want some water?'

'No, thanks. But do you have a cigarette?'

'I don't smoke,' I replied sternly. Her conduct was getting on my nerves now. She looked at the ashtray filled with cigarette stubs on the table.

'Actually, I have run out of my stock of cigarettes.'

She frowned and pursed her lips in disappointment. I had no clue where this was headed, and before I could say anything else, she opened the minibar and pulled out two bottles of beer.

She offered one to me, but I shook my head.

'Are you sure?' she confirmed, the chilled bottle still in her extended hand.

'Yes.'

'Okay!' She shrugged and gulped down the entire bottle within a minute, as if it was the last bottle of water left on earth which could satisfy her parched throat.

I couldn't stop myself from losing my temper. 'Don't you have manners?'

'Why? What's wrong with drinking a beer?' she asked half amused, her English was a blend of Bengali and Hindi dialects.

'Why would you drink the beer from *my* minibar without *my* permission?'

'Permission?' She shrugged as if this was her democratic right and I had asked the stupidest question.

'Are you here for the massage or beers and cigarettes?'

'Wait, sir ji! I am a little tired. We can start with the massage in a few minutes.' She opened her purse and pulled out a cigarette from a fresh pack. I wondered why she had asked me for one if she was carrying it anyway. She lit the cigarette and took a long puff from it. 'You know, I have never used my own cigarette with a client.'

She made me feel like the poorest man on earth, who had taken away her rightful due. I was cursing my luck when she blurted, 'I am here for only one hour.'

I checked my watch and noticed that twenty minutes of that one hour were already over.

'Will you please start the massage now? Please!' This time, I almost pleaded.

'I need advance payment.'

I opened the purse and paid her a thousand rupees, even though the logical side of my mind wanted to throw her out of the room.

'Can we start now?'

'No *tada-tadi,* babu. Go slow, sir!' she said, with a bewitching grin.

She neared me and started touching my back.

I shouted to alert her, 'Ouch! Back pain...'

'Don't worry, sir ji! I have solutions to all your problems.'

'Listen, if I fall asleep during the massage, you can finish and leave the room quietly.'

'Okay!' She put her hand on my neck and asked, 'You want only a massage?'

'Yes!'

'Where exactly do you have the pain?' She asked and started touching at various points on my back. 'Here?' she pressed slightly harder at one point and checked.

'No, slightly lower...'

'Here...?'

...and I screamed, 'Aaah, yes yes!'

4

I woke up and noticed that it was morning already. I had slept like a log through the night and fortunately, the back pain had gone down. Even though it still ached, I was able to move my back and neck with ease. There were definitely fewer screams than yesterday.

I sat up comfortably in bed and gently twisted my neck. The balm seemed to have worked wonders. My eyes landed on the ashtray. The five unfinished cigarette butts had a story to tell. And so did the empty minibar and the dustbin filled with six empty beer bottles.

I quickly opened my purse to check if I still had my cash. I relaxed immediately when I found it in its right place.

I grabbed my phone and opened Instagram to see it flooded with messages.

I posted a small video snippet of the previous day's lecture with a caption "A decent turnout and a nice interactive session". It read awkward. I edited the caption before posting the video, "Huge turnout and great interactions". I kept the phone aside and thought of satisfying my craving for coffee. Quite unexpectedly, the washroom door opened and I saw someone's shadow. It petrified me.

'Who the hell...?' I almost shouted and realised that it was her. 'Lalita, what are you doing here? I told you to leave after the massage was done.'

'Really?' She shrugged. 'You want me to go?'

'Of course!'

She came closer and sat on the bed. A whiff of beer hit my nostrils. Her deep cleavage was a little hard to ignore as she sat up close.

'Please leave or I will have to call the hotel security.'

She laughed and said, 'If you call them, then I will call the police. Then *you* will have to explain what I was doing with a rich man through the night.'

I took a deep breath. 'What do you want?'

'Where is my tip?'

'Tip? For what?' Was she kidding me!

'I spent almost five hours here and you did not even offer me a tip!' she tried to make a puppy face.

I pointed at the minibar and dustbin before asking, 'You still need a tip?'

'You are such a miser! Staying in a four-star hotel and paying me only five hundred bucks!'

'Excuse me, I have paid you a thousand rupees.'

'Fawaz gets five hundred rupees per entry in a hotel.'

'Oh!' I groaned.

It was a realisation as sharp as my back injury – how many homes were running because of my pain. I checked my wallet and found a few more hundred rupee notes.

I pulled out the notes. Her face now wore a worry line. She bent backwards, looking at the cash. I assumed she was making some calculations.

'What happened?' she asked

I shook my head.

'Am I not that attractive?' she hit out a strange question.

I looked at her deeply for the first time. I got up from the bed feeling uncomfortable with her close proximity. I slowly walked out into the balcony and asked her to join me. I lit a cigarette and offered it to her. She puffed from it like a carefree young girl. I looked at the grandeur of the hotel. Luxury has no limits, but affordability does.

'Why did you enter this field?'

'Don't ask stupid questions,' she cut me short.

'No, I am serious.'

'You don't want to hear my story.'

The seductive, enchanting Lalita suddenly changed into a silent and distant girl. I wondered how I could bring her smile back. I dug my hand into my pocket and pulled out some cash. 'I mostly use credit cards and I have only about four hundred rupees.' I extended the notes towards her. 'Sorry for disappointing you.'

She did not take the money from my hand so I walked back in and placed it on the bed.

She saw it, but did not move. Instead, she dashed into the other direction, picked up her bag, buckled up her high heels and adjusted her scarf, ready to head out.

I picked the unattended cash from the bed and called out, 'What happened?'

'Sir, I don't need your sympathy.'

5

I was anxious about the book launch later in the day. I had posted about the same on Instagram with hashtags #excited #newbook #kolkatareaders, when my phone rang.

'Good morning, Mr Arun! Starmark book store welcomes you, sir.'

'Thank you so much,' I said, clearly smitten with the cheerful reception over the phone.

'Sir, could you tell us a rough estimate of the number of readers you are expecting for the launch this evening? We will plan a seating arrangement accordingly.'

'Umm, probably fifty or sixty... I can't say for sure.'

'That should help, sir. Thank you.'

I disconnected the call and landed on my Instagram page. Close to three hundred people had seen the post and two people had commented by the time I finished the call. I took this as a good sign.

I went to the washroom and stared at the man in the mirror for a while. I looked tired and worn out, owing to the experiences of the previous day. I sprinkled some rose water on my face, applied a face pack and washed it off after half an hour.

Then I looked at my rehabilitated face again, wondering if I still needed to do such things at the age of thirty-eight. I gazed at my thinning hairline too. Sigh! It is most painful to see your rare asset falling, when you can do nothing to stop it.

I picked up one of my favourite T-shirts, sprayed a nice cologne and combed my hair. The black T-shirt went pretty well with the black jeans. I wore a brown coat on top and the mirror pointed out that I had worn the same coat to six other book launches too. I looked at myself and asked, 'Am I looking like an author?'

I realized I had spent quite a while in self-admiration and needed to make a move.

I called up the driver, 'Hi Rakesh! I am ready. Please come to the reception.'

I grabbed my artistic cotton handbag while heading out, which was mostly empty but added to my look. On my way out, I bumped into Fawaz. In fact, he came running towards me the moment he saw me, like I was his long-lost friend.

'How are you feeling now, sir?'

'Much better,' I said with a forced smile.

'Great! I am sure you had a great time.' He smiled like a pig who was sitting in a mud-pool. I did not want to spoil my mood before the launch, so I simply nodded and rushed out.

I reached the venue way before time and inferred that as an author, I should not be the first one to arrive at the scene. I decided to wait in the cab itself, and after the coordinators had called me up twice, I decided that I was late enough to be called a celebrity.

When I am restless, I have a habit of shaking my left leg. I looked at my face in the car rear-view mirror and took a deep breath, whispering to myself, 'Never surrender, Mr author!'

I was trying to guess how many people would turn up for the launch. I took the stairs to the first floor, anticipating twenty to thirty odd people. That's when I saw a heavy crowd at the entrance of the book store. A sweet lady welcomed me with a grand smile. 'Starmark welcomes you, sir.'

'Thanks,' I said with a genuine, warm smile. 'Wow! Huge turnout at the store!' I exclaimed.

I saw a podium set up for the launch on one side, and a life size billboard announcing a 60% off on some books. More than half of the girls in the crowd were hovering around it. Something died inside me; the crowd was there for the sale.

'Sir, please follow me,' gestured the event coordinator. She took me in the opposite direction of the crowd. A pyramid of my books had been created for the event, and it brought back my smile instantly. My smile didn't last for too long, though. The lady's hand brushed against the pyramid and the books came tumbling down. Everything came to a standstill for me.

I had not even recovered from the shock of the books falling when I heard the woman starting off the session. A couple of boys ran to put the pyramid in place again, and things went on as usual, as if this was an ordinary occurrence.

'A big hello to all our guests today! Please get ready to meet the author whose books have melted our hearts. Currently based in Pune, he grew up with a dream of becoming a teacher, but destiny landed him in the field of writing. Travelling to different places has taught him about different cultures and people, and makes him wonder how despite all the differences, there is a bond that unites them...'

I heard a few lines and yawned. I was hearing the same introduction for the hundredth time. Finally, after all that jazz, I was called to the stage.

The gathering looked pumped up and keen. I briefed them about my new book and discussed various things in conversation with the anchor. I also explained how this new book was different from my other works so far.

We got the same questions from the young readers that were usually asked, and I mechanically gave them the same answers that I routinely did in all other events.

'This would be the last question. Yes, that lady in the white dress,' said the anchor, giving a young girl the opportunity.

'Sir, you have written so many books on women empowerment, but you have never written about human trafficking or...' she hesitated a little before adding, 'You have not written about prostitution.'

My eyes twitched and I rubbed my forehead, as if in thought. This was too much of a coincidence and it unsettled me. I looked at the anchor with a cow face, and she sympathized with my condition.

'Sorry, time's up! For those who still want to connect with Arun sir, can ask their questions personally. You can now get your books signed.' I heaved a sigh of relief.

I signed almost sixteen to eighteen copies with 'Love, Arun Kumar' and seven with 'Never surrender in life' and two with someone's boyfriend's name. A book enthusiast came up and asked, 'Sir, would you please say hello to my girlfriend? She is a big fan of yours.'

'Sure. I would love to, but after the event.'

The signing went on, and a few people clicked pictures with me, some others taking selfies from weird angles. After close to an hour, almost everyone had left the place. I remembered the boy who had a special request. I signalled at the lover boy and he came forward with a smile.

'Can I call my girlfriend over a WhatsApp video call?'

'Sure, but only for a minute.'

'Sir, ten seconds are enough.'

I was controlling my emotions. The boy had given me a perfect fan moment. He dialled and almost shouted when she picked up, 'Hey, Mili! I am with your favourite author. Can you guess?'

He then shifted the mobile screen towards me and I caught a glimpse of the beautiful girl smiling on the other side.

'Hi Mili, how are you?'

'Wow! Hello sir, I cannot believe I am talking to you...'

Blood was rushing at double its speed in my system for the first time since landing. Now I understood why it is called 'the city of joy'.

'Sir you are looking so different. You are cuter in person,' she gushed.

At the age of thirty-eight, someone was calling me cute. I blushed.

'Sir, I am a big fan and I have read all your works.'

'All of them! Wow!' It was a moment for which an author could die.

'Yes sir, all thirteen books.'

'Really?' There was a large confusion on my face. I had written only ten till now.

I steered the conversation for clarity. 'Which one is your favourite?'

She thought for few seconds and uttered, '*Blue Suits You.*'

'It was written by Neel, not by me.'

'Oh! But you look just like Neel sir,' Mili punctured my enthusiasm.

'Ohh!' I gave the phone to the boy and glared at him.

'Hey, it is Arun sir,' he started clarifying.

'Arun Kumar?' she started squealing again. 'I am a big fan of his work. I have read all his books too, but he really looks similar to Neel sir.'

I held my head and wondered if I looked like every guy in the entire India.

6

'Could you please take me to some place where I can withdraw some cash and also buy some traditional signature sweets?' I told Rakesh as soon as I settled in the cab.

'Sure sir. I will take you to Park Street.'

We reached Park Street shortly. It was the most lavishly lit area in Kolkata. The cleanliness said that the Swachh Bharat Abhiyan had been effective in this area, because when I had visited the last time, it looked filthy. I could see branded showrooms and restaurants around fancy hotels. The Park hotel board was glowing proudly, as if it held the place together. I got down from the car and looked around. I noticed again what I had observed in my earlier visits to Kolkata – every small nook and corner either had a paan shop or a tea stall. Just the thought of tea made me walk to a nearby stall. I asked for my favourite *kulhad chai*. This was basically the Indian style tea, served in earthenware cups which contributed to its unique taste. During my trips across India, I wondered why no other city used these terracotta cups as often as Kolkata did.

After the tea, as I walked out of the ATM after withdrawing cash, I noticed that a lady was staring at me, standing just outside the gate. Initially I thought she was there to withdraw cash and was in a hurry, but she startled me with her words.

'Please hire me, young man.'

I glanced at her, taking in her middle-aged glowing face and pointed nose. The lipstick was too gaudy and the tight fitted dress was flashing her figure to me. A strange empathy ran through me.

'Which hotel, sir? I am very reasonable.'

'I am at The Park hotel.'

She neared and whispered in my ears, "Full-service, sir?'

'What comes in full service?'

'The basics – hugging, kissing, licking, blow jobs, handjobs, oral and penetration.'

My throat went dry. My ears started burning upon hearing those words, since I never thought the "service" industry could grow to such an extent.

'Why do you do this?' I asked.

'For money,' she said, in a very matter of fact tone.

'What about your respect?'

'How can a prostitute talk about respect, Babu?'

I took my purse and gave a hundred rupees to her and said, 'Sorry I cannot afford more than this.'

She almost stretched her hand to grab the cash. I dropped the note on the ground and pretended it had fallen. She bent down and picked up the cash.

'Thank you, sir. You are a nice man.'

She was smiling at having received the money, showing no hesitation. Money was clearly everything to her.

I went back to the hotel after quickly picking up the sweets, my mind elsewhere. I paced from one corner to another restlessly. I smoked three cigarettes, one after the other. I picked up my cell phone to find thirty-three notifications. Close to fifteen people had posted pictures from the book launch, tagging me. I had a few messages on the selfies with me, saying they were elated to see me. But all that aside, what grabbed my attention were the comments asking the theme of my next work.

I stood in front of the mirror and saw a man who was now struggling to think straight. Meanwhile, my brain kept going back to the morning with Lalita. I questioned myself over and over, how an escort could talk about respect.

I picked my cell phone and dialled Fawaz.

'Hello sir! How can I help you?'

'My back pain! It's back with a vengeance.'

'Oh, so you need a massage girl?' He sounded like a staunch pimp.

'Yes, but I want the same girl.'

'Seems you liked her. Let me call you back.'

I took in a sharp breath, looking around the room to make sure it was tidy. I also made some mental calculation, as I had around five thousand rupees in my wallet. Did I need more?

My thoughts were interrupted with a knock at the door. I opened the door with anticipation, but the hope soon died.

'What happened, Mr Fawaz?'

'Sir, can I come inside?'

'You are already inside the room.'

He passed an unwanted smile. 'Sir, your favourite girl has refused to come. She said, she cannot come here for just an hour.'

I frowned. 'What does she want?'

'She has given two options – either pay her for a full night for a minimum of five thousand rupees or two thousand five hundred for short-term.'

'And what is short term?'

'Two hours and one-shot.' He winked.

This man was getting on my nerves. I quickly concluded, 'Okay, I am ready to pay for short term.'

'Sir, go for the entire night! I can arrange a discount.'

My eyes narrowed with deep lines on my forehead. One look at my straight face and he understood I was annoyed. But still, he stood there, unmoved. I pulled out two hundred rupees from my pocket and gave it to him.

He smiled and walked out of the room.

My room was on the sixth floor and I had been enjoying the view throughout my stay. I picked the room key and decided to venture out to buy alcohol.

Once out of hotel grounds, I looked around and saw a huge queue of men outside a shop. I knew I was at the right place. People were shouting in Bengali and no one wanted to wait for their turn. I managed to push myself through the crowd and reached the counter.

'Six beer bottles, please,' I had to scream over the din of voices.

'Which one, sir?'

I recollected the brand which was kept in the hotel and shouted back, 'Budweiser.'

'1200 rupees.'

'Oh!' I took a few seconds and said, 'Can you make it four.'

'That will be 800 rupees.'

He packed the bottles in a black plastic bag along with a few complimentary salted chips and snacks. I was almost impressed with the gesture.

'The chips and snacks are against the change, dada."

I walked for a bit more before returning to my room. I opened the minibar, now restocked with beer. I replaced those with the ones I had just bought. I cleaned my bed and stuffed the dirty clothes inside the almirah, putting the socks and shoes in one corner. I was a little exhausted and looked at my watch. It had been more than an hour since Fawaz left.

When the doorbell rang a few minutes later, I straightened up and opened the door. Lalita was looking mesmerising in a black knee-length dress, her high heels making her appear taller than I remembered her from the last time. She had changed her hairstyle today, but the red lipstick was the same. Her makeup was louder, which made her look way older than her age.

'Do you like me that much?' was what she uttered foremost.

I nodded and welcomed her inside. 'You can sit on the sofa.'

'First, where is my advance payment?'

'Do you always think about money?'

'People have all the fun and then, they refuse to pay.'

I sighed and dug out a few currency notes. 'Two thousand for two hours, right?'

'Hmm, depends on what you want. A massage? Or something else?' she asked while stuffing the notes in her purse.

'Do you want a beer?'

'Beer?' Her eyes shone. 'Seems you are in a good mood today.'

I held the minibar open for her. 'Please help yourself.'

She looked at the stock of bottles but did not move. I prodded, 'What happened? You want something else?'

'Do you have a cigarette?'

I let go of the minibar door, and offered an entire packet to her. She almost beamed with happiness. She took out a beer on her own and finished it in one go. After which, she opened a second and offered it to me.

'No, no. I don't drink. This is for you.'

She came closer and said, 'Sir, since you've treated me so well, I promise I will treat you just as nicely.' She ran her fingers over my cheeks. 'Tell me what you want and I will charge only half.'

'Wow! Just half?'

'Yes! But can I have one more beer please?'

'Sure. But go slow.'

'So you like going slow...'

Sigh. I understood we were not on the same page.

'What do you do for a living, sir?' she said after finishing the second bottle.

'I am a writer.'

'Wow! What do you write?'

'Stories of love.'

'Hmm, what kind of love? There is no love!' She smiled.

'You are already two beers down, I am not sure if you can understand my love stories.'

She took a deep breath and sat on the sofa. She pulled up her legs onto the sofa and threw her head back on the armrest. Then, she put her left palm on her breast and pretended to squeeze it seductively. She bit her lips and pouted. She looked like a struggling porn artist who was ready for masturbation. I was unmoved and smiled inwardly at her silly attempt.

'Looks like you are interested in something else?' she said.

I nodded. 'Could you please tell me a story?'

'Story? What kind of story?' She had finished her third beer by now and extended her hand for the fourth one.

'I want to know your story.'

Her face suddenly lost the smile she had pasted there. 'No no, it will make me emotional. And then, it will be difficult for me to give other services.'

'That's okay. This is all I wish to spend time on with you.'

'Why are you interested in my story?'

'Because I am a writer.'

She scanned me from top to bottom and went back to the sofa, stretching her half-naked leg on the armrest of the sofa.

'But on one condition.'

'Which is?'

'That you will not show any sympathy towards me.'

'Sympathy is also a form of love.'

'No! Today you will sympathize with me and commit something unpractical, and tomorrow, I will be a burden on you, and then...you will leave me.'

'I might start loving you.'

She smiled.

'Love and sympathy are different,' I said.

'Really? And how so?'

'Sympathy makes us realize that we are human. Love makes us a better human.'

7

In Lalita's own words

I was born in a small village near Asansol. My father was working as a clerk in the post office. We had enough to live with dignity. Since I was their only child, we managed things pretty well. I was closer to my mother emotionally, though I loved Baba a lot too. In short, we were a small and lovable family.

I went to a Bengali-medium government school about five kilometres from our house. I had to go there because the only other option was to sit at home.

Then, one tragic night, I lost my father. He had mistakenly consumed toxic alcohol. My life became a struggle from that day. Even though my mother received some money as a provident fund beneficiary, our regular income was gone. But we continued living in the same house as my *mama-mami* stayed close by, and mom and I felt safer with them around.

I had cleared class tenth in a couple of years, but the closest intermediate school was thirty kilometres from our town. I joined the school, but not the classes. I was advised to appear just for the exams rather than having to travel for classes every day. Half the course curriculum was now in English, so I was struggling to keep pace with the other students.

It was also the time that everyone started hinting subtly at my marriage. It gave me goosebumps. I would sit in front of the mirror for hours and often imagine myself in those sparkling dresses. Since I did not know much about the outside world, I wished to become a beautiful bride myself. I would go to shops selling cosmetics, exploring the new products they had. Even though I had always been fair-complexioned, I wanted to look exactly like those models on cosmetics brand posters.

I guess I wanted to look fairer or I was obsessed, I don't know. I had once purchased a beauty cream by looking at the beautiful picture of Yami Gautam on the cover of that product. The brand claimed to make people fairer in just a few weeks. After a few trials, I understood that fairness creams and cosmetics are tools to earn money as they do not make miracles happen.

In my exploration and obsession with makeup, I had acquired a decent knowledge of cosmetics and their use. I got the job of an assistant makeup artist at a beauty parlour, but it was far off from the village. My work eventually led me to travel to different places for bridal makeup and other salon services. It was like being in a dream profession.

There was a photo studio adjacent to the parlour. I would often go to the studio to help ladies dress up for the photoshoot. My work was slowly getting acknowledged by my customers and I came to be known as 'Lalita, the magical beautician'.

But on the flip side, this paused my education, even though I always wanted to study further. Between two different dreams, I opted for the easier one.

Around this time, I met Mukesh. He worked at the photo studio as a freelancer. His attractive personality and charming ways got to me. He travelled to various places, especially to villages, for work. His camera gallery was flooded with pictures of beautiful ladies. Once, while working with a common client, I requested him to take my picture too. I had looked at my picture in his camera over and over again. I looked so pretty. It was the first time someone had made me look that beautiful.

Life was going well, but then my mother started staying sick. I was nineteen and did not know how to go about getting her medical help. She was diagnosed with jaundice and her condition was serious as per our local doctor. We hopped from hospital to hospital in bigger towns, which drained my earnings and savings at a rapid pace.

I took loans from people I knew, even the parlour owner lent me some money, but that was not enough. My only family and love, my mom, was dying with every passing day and it broke me.

The money I had taken from others was exhausted soon and I didn't know where to go for help. The relatives had been helpful, but they had their own constraints. In that crunch, Mukesh helped me with a large portion of money. He was in the hospital with me, all the time. He was there when I needed someone the most and I started falling in love with him.

By god's grace, my mom finally recovered. The doctors warned me that she needed to be taken good care of and her being out of danger was the happiest news for me.

Two weeks after she came home, my mom invited Mukesh over for a meal. She wished to introduce him to mamaji. He asked various questions related to Mukesh's family and past work, but he kept making excuses and avoided sharing any details. I guess I was lost enough in his love to see anything amiss as he had won my trust in helping me with mom. Eventually, I couldn't resist his charm anymore and we made love. I was terrified, since it was my first time. But he handled me so well that I could guess that he had done this many times in the past. Nevertheless, I accepted it as his past and dreamt of a better future with him.

One evening, I was sitting with mom when she started talking about my marriage plans. I came clean about my feelings for Mukesh.

'Mom, I love a boy.'

'I know that, but his reputation is bad.'

'But no one knows him better than me, Ma,' I tried to reason with her.

My mom went silent and I was distressed that she couldn't see my feelings for him.

That night, I was struggling to sleep when mom came into my room.

'Do you love him so much?' she whispered to me.

'Yes, Ma,' I replied confidently.

'There is a basic problem in your love,' she said.

'What, Ma?'

'I guess you feel indebted to him as he helped your mother during a tough time.'

'So what, Ma?'

'He sympathized with you in your tough time.'

'Sympathy is another form of love, Ma.'

'Sympathy cannot stay lifelong, and one day, you could become a burden. Kindness eventually fades away.'

'I will never let anyone sympathize with me and take advantage.' I held her hand and promised.

'You are the only one I have. I will be happy if you are happy.'

I hugged my mom and promised to myself that I'd make her proud. I was euphoric to share the news with Mukesh, but he had gone to Kolkata for some work.

When he returned a couple of days later, my excitement was reduced by the apprehensions on his face.

'What happened?'

'My friend's boss's family needs a nurse for a few months. They have asked me to help.'

'Oh! What happened suddenly?'

'They had an accident and there's nobody to care for them. They need temporary support, that's all.'

'Hmm! How many months do they need a nurse for?' I asked, rummaging my brain for anyone who could fit the requirement.

'Two months, maximum.'

'Okay! Did you find someone?'

'Not yet.' He shook his head. Then, he looked at me with a smile and I shrugged. 'Would you help me through this?'

I couldn't make head or tail out of his proposal. 'I am not a nurse! I don't even know what to do.'

'We will teach you everything.'

'No no, I cannot leave the job and my mother like that.'

'But you will get twenty-five thousand per month, and free food and accommodation.'

That had hit at the right spot. I was hesitant about leaving my mother, but I knew the value of money too well.

'Can you give me a day's time to think about it?'

'Sure, but we need to leave tomorrow itself if you're interested. Otherwise, they will find someone else.'

I was overwhelmed by a series of conflicting sentiments. I wanted to help him, but I did not want to leave my mother. I wanted the money, but that would delay all my life plans and I'd have to leave my job.

'Do you trust me?' he asked, extending his hand to me

'Yes.' I held his hand in mine.

He kissed my forehead, thanking me for helping him out and also promising me that we will see better times together after these two months.

Then, as a concern, he added, 'Don't tell your mom that I have advised you to work as a nurse for money. Just tell her that you need to go to the city for a better job or a beautician training or something.'

I nodded. I took his advice and convinced my mom that I was going to the city for further training in my job and would return in a couple of months.

Mukesh helped me pack as we had to leave the next day. He passed a bundle of instructions as to what I should pack. I had only one phone, which he suggested giving to mom. It was an obvious choice since it meant that I could call her anytime from anywhere.

'Make sure you tell your mom that you won't be available on phone calls for a couple of days, okay?' he instructed.

'Why?' I wondered.

'It's a new city for you. Plus, you will need to first purchase another phone and then, a SIM card. That could take a while.'

I nodded but wasn't sure why we couldn't use public phones. I could always use his phone, I told myself and forgot about it.

I hugged my mom before leaving. I hugged her for the last time. She whispered something in my ears that echoed in my mind all through my journey.

'Live a life of self-respect. When you respect yourself, others will respect you.'

Mad rush at the Kolkata railway station welcomed me into the city. Though many prominent names are associated with the city – such as Mother Teresa, Rabindranath Tagore, Satyajit Ray and Subhash Chandra Bose – I had only read about Kolkata in books.

'Why is it called the "city of joy"?' I asked Mukesh.

'Because everyone is happy here,' he replied nonchalantly.

We hired a cab and it crossed Eden Gardens. The ground was much bigger than I remembered seeing on TV. Our journey had begun from Dum Dum in the north and continued to Park Street and the Esplanade, and further onto Tollygunge in the south. Then, we landed at a very filthy lane where our lodge was located. It was a small but presentable lodge.

He was not in a hurry to visit his friend's boss's place. I was so lost in looking around and soaking in the new city that I did not ask about the job or his friend.

In the evening, we went for a stroll and enjoyed some roadside food, relishing the panipuri and rasgullas. We also went to have a look at the Victoria Memorial. It was a memorable day for me, exploring Kolkata with the one I loved.

The next morning, Mukesh asked me to wear the white Bengali saree which he had advised me to bring from home.

'Is it a nurse requirement?' I questioned curiously.

'Everyone wants a beautiful nurse.' He smiled.

I draped the saree and topped it with makeup, of which I was an expert. I applied a coffee-brown lipstick because I loved that shade and it was subtle.

Mukesh took a look at me and immediately pointed, 'Why don't you apply red lipstick?'

I raised my eyebrows and he took me in an embrace, telling me I looked lovely in red. Too deeply in love to question, I nodded and changed the lip colour shade.

I guess trust and stupidity have no boundaries.

We took a taxi till Kalighat and after a few minutes, the taxi stopped outside a temple. We did not go inside, but walked to one side. There were narrow lanes and a taxi couldn't have come in anyway. Filthy sewage was flowing on the sides of the road, but finally, we landed outside a decent six-storey building. The houses and roads seemed ordinary. Mukesh had not said a word since the driver had dropped us.

We climbed up to the sixth floor. My heart was racing and Mukesh's silence was making me uncomfortable. He knocked at the door and a fat lady opened the door a few seconds later.

'Oh, Salim!' The lady greeted Mukesh. She had a heavy build and her blouse buttons were about to explode with the tension around her bosom. Her big bindi and red lipstick showed that she had a poor sense of makeup.

'Namaste ji,' I said.

She nodded and we went inside.

As soon as the lady was out of our hearing range, I asked Mukesh, 'Who is Salim?'

Mukesh whispered back, 'That's my nickname.'

I was slightly taken aback, but the lady returned. Mukesh introduced me to her, 'She is Lalita and she would be working as a nurse.'

'*Mashallah,* she is beautiful,' she said scanning me.

She introduced herself as Rani. I sat at the edge of the sofa and looked around the house. It was a big house and there were three closed doors. I guessed one of them might belong to the patient.

Rani came from the kitchen with glasses of water. I took a sip of water and saw Mukesh signalling something to Rani. An obdurate numbness ran through me.

'Do you know how to give an injection?' the lady asked.

I shook my head in negative.

She looked at Mukesh. 'No! She is not a professional nurse, but we can teach her, right?'

'Yes, you go and bring some medicines and injection. I will take care of things from here.'

'What about the money for the medicines?'

She passed a cunning smile and offered a bundle of cash. I wondered whether the medicines were so expensive or something else was going on.

Mukesh started to walk towards the door.

'Where are you going? Don't leave me alone,' I said weakly, not knowing what else to say.

'Relax! I'll be right back with the medicines.' He closed his eyes for a second and his jaw fell. There were traces of regret on his face, but he quickly rushed out of the door whispering, 'Take care.'

I was trying to connect the missing dots. In the meanwhile, the lady neared me and started patting my head, just like we do with a pet. She opened one of the doors and called me inside. I walked behind her foolishly. Two men were sitting inside, and it seemed that they were waiting for me.

'New maal?' one of them asked.

'Yes, but she is fresh. We'd need to train her,' Rani replied.

I crossed my hands over my chest and fidgeted a little. I tried to move back, but Rani pulled me in and closed the door.

'Who brought her?'

'Salim.'

'He is an expert in catching fresh pieces.' The man guffawed.

I stood stupefied like a brainless animal, sweating profusely.

'We need to do a photoshoot. Get ready!' Rani said to me and opened a small almirah. She showed me some dresses.

I couldn't think of anything else, so I joined my hands and pleaded, 'Please let me go.'

I could guess they had played this game in the past, because the moment I said this, one of the men lifted me on his shoulder and dumped me on the bed. I did not notice the physical pain at all. I guess I was shocked and terrified.

Rani almost roared, 'Salim has sold you here for a hefty amount and now you are in business. The day you earn double the amount we have paid for you, we will let you go.'

I went silent and tried to comprehend her words. So, I was sold! Tears came rushing along with the realisation.

'You have to sleep with people and smile dear. Nobody pays for tears.' Rani broke my trance.

I kept wondering why I had naively believed everything Mukesh said, all the promises he made. Were all of them fake? I had gone so numb that I could not show much resistance. The pain in my heart was deeper than any physical wounds they could give me.

'You will get nothing till you are ready for the photoshoot,' Rani threatened as everyone moved out. They did not give me anything to eat or drink for a long time. I sat silently for the first few hours and then I started crying. I cried for hours, thinking of my mother, how she had warned me against Mukesh... no, Salim... or whatever his real name was. I looked outside the small window, the only source of ventilation, thinking of jumping out of the window. But it was too small, and I was on the sixth floor. I spent an entire day lying on the bed like a dead body. Then, the door opened. Rani walked in, trying to convince me.

'Listen, it will be painful initially, I agree, but you will start liking it after that.'

'What will you do with my photos?' I asked.

'We will send it to some good people. They have a lot of money, but no company. No wife or girlfriend.'

She was explaining how her work was a form of social service. Then she gave me a glass of water which I drank in one go. She helped me get into a knee-length dress and emphasised that a bright coloured lipstick, kajal and open hair were an absolute essential.

She clicked few pictures before suggesting I change into the red T-shirt and short pants. The last ensemble was a saree without the blouse.

Finally, my portfolio was ready. I looked at those pictures in the camera and tears welled up.

On the third day, she came into the room, excited. 'You are lucky! A rich guy has made a booking for you.'

'No! I am not ready,' was all I could say before she screamed and two people walked in.

She instructed them, 'Make sure she gets ready!'

The man slapped me across the face, but Rani intervened, 'Are you an idiot! Don't hit on the face!'

That day I got to know the real worth of my face. They had brought along a plastic pipe. They beat me till I said, 'I am ready.'

I wore a short black dress and matching high heels. I took a step, only to be pushed out by Rani. She yelled at me to put on some makeup too. With Rani standing over my head, I was forced to darken the kohl and the red lipstick. With a bronzed make-up effect, I looked like a cheaper version of a catalogue model. She instructed Aslam to drop me. Before heading for my first client call I asked, 'How much did you pay to Mukesh for me?'

'Mukesh? Oh, Salim! One lakh rupees.'

'How much would you need to let me go?'

'Two lakhs!'

'If I fail to get those two lakh rupees, then?'

'Then also we will leave you after two years, if you wish to go.'

That gave me a ray of hope.

'Although, to be honest, I have not seen anyone leave this business after two years.' She smirked.

A fancy handbag was given to me, along with a phone. Rani told me outgoing calls and messages were barred from it. I was to be escorted to the guesthouse and Aslam would wait outside till I got free.

Just as I was leaving, Rani passed one last instruction.

'If the guest asks anything, just say no one has touched you before and you are a virgin.'

I had spent my first night with a senior government official. I was a bait for a middle-aged rich man. I came out of the guest house and saw two men waiting for me. They escorted me to that hell once again. I looked at my face in the mirror and closed my eyes. I could not look at myself in the eyes.

In the days that followed, I was always escorted everywhere. There was not a moment when I was alone. I decided that before putting an end to my life, I had to fulfil my last wish.

'Can I call my mom?' I asked Rani.

'I told you, it's not allowed.'

'Why?'

'Don't ever question my decisions.'

'Why?'

The answer was a sound slap.

'Please let me talk to her once. I will talk to her in front of you,' I tried to convince her.

She slapped me again and I went silent.

'Did you never miss your mother?'

She looked straight at me before closing her eyes for a few seconds. Her expression mellowed a little. 'I will allow you, if you make today's client happy.'

I understood that the next client was an important person for them.

I nodded and thought I would go through this ordeal just one more time before I die. I was taken to The Park hotel and after a few security checks, was guided to a big suite. I had never seen such a beautiful room in my life. There were flower vases everywhere and the carpet was shining with golden embroidery. There was a big TV screen that made one section of the room look like a mini theatre.

I saw my client and was shocked to find a leading minister of that area. I had seen him giving long moral speeches on television. I lost all respect for him, so I could only respond with my fake smiles and no-resistance sex.

He said in a tone of disappointment, 'You are only as good as ice.'

'Sorry, I tried my best.'

'You look distraught. What happened?' he asked while pouring himself a drink.

'Actually, I am missing my mom.'

There was a silence in the room. Then, for the first time, he did not look at me like I was a doll that he had bought. The word 'mother' still touches us somewhere, I guess; it makes us feel alive and human.

'You want to talk to your mother?'

I folded my hands, unable to contain my feelings. Silent tears fell from my eyes.

'Okay, I will dial her number. Tell me!' He dialled the number and nobody picked up. I looked at him and he dialled again. After the third attempt, someone answered.

'Hello mamaji! How are you?'

'Who, Lalita?'

The minister signalled for me to go to the balcony and talk.

'Where is mom, mamaji?'

'She is hospitalized with jaundice again, Lalita,' his voice cracked.

'So, you are in the same government hospital that we took her to?' My heart raced at the thought.

'No, the government hospital doctor advised us to go for a bigger hospital, but...'

'But, money is the issue,' I completed. 'You can sell off all the gold.'

'We already sold most of it.'

'How much money do you need for the treatment?'

'Some ten thousand rupees immediately, but close to one lakh rupees within a week.'

'You don't even have ten thousand, mamaji?'

'Beti, we have already invested close to two lakhs, and now we need another ten thousand urgently.'

'I will do something mamaji.' My mind was racing, just like my heart. 'Could you please share the account details?'

'Sure.'

'Where is Mom? Can I hear her voice?'

'Yes, just a minute!' He handed the phone to my mom and her feeble voice came through.

'How are you, my Lalita?'

She sounded ecstatic to hear my voice. 'I am happy, mom,' I said with moist eyes.

'How is your beautician training going?'

'Good! I am learning a lot of new things.' I couldn't tell her I was going to end my life after this last call to her.

'Don't worry about anything, maa. I will arrange for all the money you need.'

'I'm proud of you, beti. God bless you!'

I disconnected the call and came back into the room. Not knowing who else I could ask, I approached the MLA. 'Sir, can you help me with some money?'

He shot a strange look at me and I explained the situation.

'What's in it for me?' he asked with a crooked smile.

'I can give you what you want.'

'I am already done with you'

'Has anyone ever given you a blow job with ice cream?'

He raised his eyebrows and bit his lips. There was a spark in his eyes.

'If you make me happy, I will give you the money.'

I knelt down, unbuttoning his shorts. Then, I closed my mind and whispered to myself, 'Mom, I will not let you die.'

8

Lalita finished her story. There was pin drop silence in the room. She went to the balcony to smoke. I counted my life struggles and they felt so small in front of Lalita's challenges. I looked at the fourth beer bottle, still half-filled. She had stopped drinking the beer somewhere in the middle of telling her story.

I went after her and noticed that there were tears in her eyes. She closed her eyes tight when she saw me approaching. I understood that I should leave her alone.

I went to the washroom and quickly washed my face. When I finally looked up into the mirror, I saw a selfish man. I hated him. In looking for a real story, he had used an innocent girl. I sat on the toilet seat and walked out from the washroom only after fifteen minutes.

'Sir, my time is up! Can I go now?' Lalita asked me as soon as she saw me come out of the washroom.

'No! Be here for another hour and I will pay you extra.'

'Don't waste your money on me,' Lalita said as she picked up her bag from the table.

'No, I need you.' My voice came out as a plea.

'You are not interested in sex and I am in no mood to give you a massage. So I should just go.'

'Oh come on! I need you for my...'I was at a loss of words.

'...entertainment?' Lalita completed my sentence.

'No! After hearing your story, I don't think I can get any sleep.'

'Okay, I'll stay. But I have one condition.'

'Oh, anything.'

'No more hunting for my past.'

'Agreed! From now on, I would only talk about the future.'

'Done.' She finally smiled a little.

'Have you ever tried a four-star hotel's restaurant?'

'No, I have been to quite a few rooms, though.'

'Would you like to try?' I asked and she looked straight up. 'Coffee?'

She nodded.

I dialled the reception to check whether the hotel restaurant was open.

'No sir, it's close to 2 a.m. and all the restaurants are closed. They reopen at 6.30 a.m. for breakfast. You can order room service in the meantime, sir,' the receptionist answered politely.

'Hmm. I want to sit at a good place. Can you suggest something?'

'Sir, if you wish to have light snacks and beverages, you can try the rooftop swimming area. The pinnacle top café is open twenty-four hours.'

'Okay, thanks!'I ended the call and said in a euphoric voice to Lalita, 'Let's go to the rooftop bar. Just me and you.'

She smiled. 'Can I use the washroom?'

I nodded.

While she was away, I opened my wallet and counted the cash. There were another two thousand rupees left. There was a credit card which gave me temporary confidence, but was surely going to give me a permanent headache later.

Lalita walked out of the washroom and I was surprised to see the new version. Gone was the makeup, the obnoxiously loud lipstick and her face showcased a genuine happiness. She looked relaxed. I picked the cigarette box and room key before walking towards the lift.

'How many times have you come to this hotel?'

'Some ten to twelve times.'

We reached the rooftop café on the ninth floor.

The ambience there was sparkling. The blue sky was interspersed with white fluffy cotton wool clouds. The rippling slivers of the water, as much as everything around, filled me with buoyant energy. The area was fairly empty, with just one couple sitting in one corner, holding their respective drinks. The restaurant gave out a magnificent view of the city. I was welcomed to the table in the centre of the café and the bartender gave a strange look to Lalita. It seemed he had seen her before.

'Do you like the place?' I tried to divert her attention.

'Yes, it's nice.' She looked excited. She took the menu and started reading through.

'Wow! Coffee here is four hundred rupees? Plus taxes!'

'Don't worry about that.' I smiled. 'Whatever time we have left, let's talk about something positive.'

Her lips curved into a smile.

Just then, she got a few notifications on her phone and she was suddenly upset. I felt the need to divert her mind and asked, 'Okay, so, who do you hate the most in life?'

Just as I said the question out loud, I realised my mistake. Luckily, I was saved because the waiter walked towards us with our coffee. I mentally scolded myself. How could I have started the conversation with hate!

But Lalita had already heard my question as she answered almost immediately. 'I hate men,' she said, looking at the waiter.

I took her answer silently, without seeking any explanation.

'Suppose today is your last day on earth, what will you do?' I asked.

'I will live like rich people do.'

'Seriously! Only money comes to your mind?'

'Yes sir! I am losing my self-respect for money every single day.'

'So, money would bring back the respect?'

'Yes.'

I smiled and passed a supportive expression. 'Others want money for luxury and you want money for respect?'

'Yes. With money... Oh, that reminds me, I need to call someone.'

'Your boyfriend?'

'No, a business associate. He is one of the few guys I don't hate much, because he gives me business.'

Her explanation gave away that she was talking about some pimp. There was a lump in my throat. She moved a little far from the table and started talking in Bengali. I tried hard to hear what she was saying. '*Ami bhalo achhi ar panch sho taka apnake kal diye debo.*' I failed to understand Bengali beyond the basic phrases.

I frowned at her when she came back. 'I told him that I'm safe and the customer has paid me extra money. And I will pay his commission tomorrow.'

'A part of all this goes to him as well?' I wondered what she'd be making, because now I knew two men were taking their cut.

'Yes, of course.'

'But why?'

'He arranges business for me and manages the safety angle. Like, if someone complains to the police or there's any kind of harassment, he saves me from all that.'

'Who is he? Some kind of local don?'

'No, he is just like Robin Hood.'

'You know about Robin Hood?'

'Not really. He asks me to call him that and he dreams of becoming a politician someday.'

'Politics and prostitution have to be the few jobs where inexperience is considered a virtue,' I said and took the last sip of my coffee.

'So, the coffee is finished.' Her voice echoed that her dream was over, and now she needed to get back to reality.

I couldn't stop myself from asking, 'Did you ever think of leaving this business?'

'Who would accept us, sir?'

It felt like a challenge. My tongue was stuck in my parched mouth and I was still thinking of something I could say.

'Ok, would you accept a prostitute?' she asked me, piercing my eyes with her gaze.

Prostitute! I had heard the word in movies and had a fixed image in my head. I observed her and tried to figure out why she was so different? Why had she been identified as a prostitute? Anyone could have done the same thing in the given circumstances. For me, a prostitute is a respectable lady who chooses to live, as against dying at the hands of tough circumstances.

The emotions in my heart must have started to reflect on my face. I wanted to say something, but couldn't formulate the right words. The mobile reminder diverted my attention. It read, *Departure for airport.*

We were now the only ones who were making the sole waiter work. I signalled and he came running with the bill. I made the payment and we left for my room.

I packed my clothes, a few books and the charger. I did not have many things to pack anyway. But still, Lalita helped me. There was satisfaction on her face, but I was feeling helpless.

'Can I have your mobile number?' I asked, to which she nodded.

I saved her number and checked, 'You don't want mine?'

'No. I want to live in the reality.'

I took in a deep breath. 'So, now what?'

'When will you be back in Kolkata?'

'Maybe for the next book launch. Not before that.'

'Nice! Would you write a story about us?'

'I don't think so.'

'Why?'

'I write hopeful stories.'

We both understood the realities of life and honestly, who were we fooling!

She sought permission to use the washroom again and spent longer than required. I lit a cigarette while waiting for her. I was getting impatient and I called the taxi driver. He assured that he'd reach in another twenty minutes.

She came out of the washroom, her puffy eyes and red nose tip explaining why she had taken so long.

'The bathroom tap isn't working properly,' she reported.

'No worries! I am leaving anyway.'

With nothing else coming to mind, I offered, 'Listen, my driver can drop you. It is 4 a.m. and might be tough for you to get a taxi.'

'No sir. I will get a taxi myself or I will call my friend.'

I thought of saying some inspirational sign-off line, but I drew a blank. She neared me, stretching her arm a little. I hugged her and closed my eyes. I did not notice the smell or feel of her skin. I was at a standstill. We parted, out eyes smiling through the tears.

'You are a good man,' she said and walked out.

9

I sat on the bed and closed my eyes after Lalita left. I wanted to experience peace for a few minutes. I had just picked up the phone to update the hotel reception about my check-out when my mobile vibrated with a message.

Dear Guest, This is a customer service message from IndiGo Airlines. Your flight is delayed by two hours because of technical issues. Sorry for the inconvenience caused.

I called the taxi driver and informed him about the delay. I thought of taking a power nap for an hour because I hadn't slept at all. I went to the washroom, but there was no leaking tap. My eyes opened wide on seeing the bundle of cash which was kept close to the soap dish.

'Did she forget the money?'

Then, I recollected that she had kept the money in her purse as soon as I had handed it to her yesterday. I also remembered how much that cash mattered to her. I picked up the notes and felt very insignificant. My soul was scolding me for being so self-centred.

I picked up my phone and dialled her. 'Hi Lalita! Can you come back to my room?'

'Why?'

'My flight is late and...'

'You are wasting your time, sir,' she said.

'No, I wanted to discuss something important. Can you please come?'

She disconnected the call. I sat back on the bed, resting my aching back. I was still looking at the stack of notes she had left behind. We can conquer any fear if we make up our mind, because fear exists only in our mind.

When the doorbell rang a few minutes later, I invited her in.

'What happened, author saab?'

'I have a proposal for you.'

She frowned, more confused than ever.

'Would you like to leave this business and start a new life?'

'Don't show me a dream that cannot be fulfilled.'

'Just answer me, please.'

'Yes! But how?'

'Do you trust me?'

'No! I lost everything by trusting a man.'

'All men are not the same.'

'Maybe, but I have lost faith in people.'

'Okay! But think about this. You have nothing to lose.'

She smiled and I did not wait for the answer. 'Do you have any ID card?'

'Yes, I have an Aadhaar card. We aren't allowed in if we don't show it at the hotel reception.'

'That's nice.'

'Can you make a cup of coffee for me while I plan this better?'

She nodded instantly.

'Will your Robin Hood friend create any problem for us?'

'Yes! He could file a false police complaint against you.'

'Why?'

'To punish you for taking away his regular income.'

'Hmm...'

I had cooked some plans on paper. I drafted details in my mind and thanked myself for reading thriller novels. Then, I called the taxi driver and said, 'Hey Rakesh, your services are not required. One of my friends is coming to meet me and he will drop me till the airport.'

After disconnecting the call, I went back to figuring out the details.

'Listen carefully, Lalita! You need to go out and spend some time at the reception. Maybe ask something random at the reception, but make sure your face is captured by the CCTV.'

'Why?'

'This will give the idea that you have left the place, alone.'

She nodded.

'Great, so you leave now and I will join you in another twenty minutes or so.'

'Okay, I will wait outside.'

She got up to go when I stopped her. 'Wait!'I opened my bag and pulled out a T-shirt and pyjama. 'You go to a public toilet and change into these.' Handing her the bathroom slippers, I asked her to get rid of her high heels too.

'Are you sure you want to do this for me?'

'This is not about you. It is about me.'

Lalita had left and I had twenty minutes to fix things.

I called the only person I knew in the hotel.

'Hi, Fawaz!'

'Hello sir!' he said in a sleepy tone.

'Sorry for calling you at this time.'

'No worries, sir.'

'I was about to check out and thought of thanking you personally.'

'I will be there in a few minutes.' I had hit the bull's eye, and Mr Fawaz came to see me in ten minutes.

There was no sign of sleep on his face now and he seemed to be too excited for feedback.

'How was the massage girl?'

'She just left.'

'Nice! She stayed the entire night?'

'Yes! She was such a delight,' I replied like a horny con man. 'And thanks for arranging everything'.

'My pleasure, sir. Please allow me to take your luggage to the reception area.'

I politely denied but he accompanied me till the reception anyway.

'I wanted to gift you something before I left.'

'No need for that, sir,' Fawaz said with a huge grin.

I looked at my purse and almost picked two hundred-rupees notes. The Gandhi on the note was not smiling, just like me. Before I could hand them to Fawaz, he blurted, 'Next time, try two massage girls at a time. We normally call them four hands.'

'Four hands?'

'You cannot imagine the fun when you have seductive girls on both sides.'

I realized that Fawaz was playing the incorrect cards to the wrong man. I kept one note back and gave only one hundred rupees to him. He made a face on seeing that.

'Don't worry! Next time, I will pay you more.' I winked. 'Four hands.'

I handed the room key over at the reception, looked at the CCTV camera and walked out of the hotel.

I booked a local taxi. I avoided taking Ola or Uber. Lalita was standing at the roadside a few metres away.

My oversized lower and T-shirt were too baggy for her, like a big gown hanging on a steel hanger. She looked like any other girl without the red lipstick and makeup.

We sat in the car and I directed the driver to take us to the airport. The driver took a few turns and before he could take the highway, Lalita asked, 'Can we take this lane?'

'Ma'am this road goes through the famous red-light area, Sonagachi.'

I shrugged and she made a puppy face. 'Driver, let's follow madam's instructions.'

As we neared the red light area, Lalita's expression changed. She opened her bag and pulled out a few bangles, cosmetics and lipsticks. To my surprise, she threw them all on the road and whispered, 'I am done! Please drive to the airport now.'

10

'Are we going by a flight?' Her smile overshadowed everything else on her face. I saw my excitement from the first flight journey reflected in her. It was an early morning flight, the cheapest one, and I hadn't slept for a minute.

I booked a ticket for Lalita on the same flight as mine. We walked to the check-in counter. Many eyes were scanning her, thanks to the awkward clothes. But she had learned the art of avoiding people.

'Wow! Kolkata airport is so beautiful.'

I only smiled in response.

'Are all the airports like this?'

I nodded.

She held my hand while walking to the lobby. I tried to ignore it, knowing well she was nervous as hell. We were done with the security check and the clock in the waiting area showed one hour for the boarding to start. She was scanning every passenger and their fancy bags.

'Come, I will show you my books in WHSmith!'

'WS Smit?' She couldn't pronounce the name.

'It's a kind of modern bookstore,' I explained.

We reached outside the store and there was an A4-size poster on the wall displaying a picture of me and my books. My books were stacked on one side of the table, one pile up solely for the latest release. She picked one book and flipped through a few pages. Then, she looked up at the poster on the wall.

'Is that you?' she pointed towards the poster.

I nodded, fascinated with her reaction. Every time I came to Kolkata, the airport store visit was a must.

The store manager recognized me and extended his hand. 'How are you, sir?'

Lalita was standing just behind me and the store person gaped at her. I understood that he was more curious about her.

'Meet my friend, Lalita.'

He folded his hands and said, 'Namaste, ma'am.' She beamed at the gesture.

Respect and recognition have no substitute. But she did not reply properly. She lacked training in social etiquette. The manager took me to the book-corner to get some copies of my books signed. I started signing the copies while Lalita stood at the other end, reading out aloud the titles of my books. '*The Best Wife, The Best Friend* and *A Beautiful Girl...*' she continued to flip through the pages. I finished with the book signing, thanked the store manager and walked towards the boarding gate, Lalita following me closely.

'Wow! Seems like you are a celebrity.'

I laughed. The world lives in an illusion and I did not correct her.

We finally boarded the flight.

'You can sit there,' I offered pointing to the window seat.

She was on a marathon of exploration. She was thrilled about how a plane ran on the runway. Sometimes, she looked at a foreigner who was walking restlessly and sometimes she stared at the flight attendants. She noticed their hairstyles closely, and how they spoke. I guess she liked the entire appeal of an air hostess.

She held my hand as the plane took off and kept gazing outside the window. The plane hovered above the city of joy after a few minutes.

'Wow, Kolkata is so beautiful... like I have seen in movies.'

'Can you recognize any place from up here?'

'Yes! That is Victoria Memorial,' she said pointing out the massive white building. 'I never thought the city would look so small from the top.'

'When you explore the world, you would realize we are all so insignificant compared to the entire universe.'

She came a little closer to me and rested her head on my shoulder. I gathered she was slipping into a different dream, so I shifted a little bit and asked, 'How were my books? Did you like any of them?'

She shook her head. Honestly, I was a little taken aback.

'What! You did not like my books? None of them?'

'No! There were no photos in them. Only the cover was colourful.'

'Photos? It's not a picture book.'

'Who reads so much, and that too in English!' She made a face and I laughed. 'So, what is the plan now? And where will I stay in Pune?'

'For now, you could stay at my house and...' Before I could complete, she asked another question.

'Who all are there in your family?'

'No one. Only me.'

The smile on her face widened and I thought it was time to clear out any misunderstandings.

'Actually, I will arrange something for you. I have a friend who can help us shift you to the best women rehabilitation shelter or *Nari Sudhar Kendra*.'

'What is a women rehabilitation shelter?'

'It is a live-in campus for women who have left or wish to leave the business they were forced into. The members of the shelter will educate you and help you re-establish your life.'

'All prostitutes go there?'

'Lalita, call a fool a fool and an intelligent person intelligent, but always call a prostitute a lady.'

'Oh!' She groaned

'Is there a problem?'

'No, I thought you have accepted me.'

'Yes! I have accepted you as... a friend '

'Friend... But I am a girl?'

'So what?'

'I never thought a boy and a girl can be friends.'

'Friendship is one of the purest relationships.'

'So, am I your *girl*-friend?'

I laughed.

11

When we landed in Pune, I felt safer. I never believed it could be so easy to get her away from that world, or maybe it was too early to conclude that. I wondered how many girls would still be stuck in that hellhole. I dropped my bag in a corner as soon as I entered the house.

Lalita looked around the house and sat on the plastic chair. The kitchen was messy and a few drops of oil had spilt onto the floor. I looked at those and realized that they had been there for a long time.

'Can I make some tea?' she asked.

'Yes! I was thinking the same.'

'You relax. Let me make the tea.'

'Ok!' I showed her where the tea and sugar were kept, while asking, 'How is the house?'

'I have not explored it completely. What is in there?' she pointed to one of the closed rooms.

'Nothing is in there. It belongs to the landlord and I don't have access to it. Only this room, the kitchen and balcony have been rented out to me.'

She looked lost and pointed at the other door.

'So, is that the washroom?' I nodded my affirmation.

'So, you have only one room?'

'Yes, one room and one washroom.'

'You live in a rented flat?'

I nodded.

'I thought you are a rich man.'

'I told you I am an author.'

Her shoulders had drooped and she licked her lips. We sat in the balcony, the part of the house I loved. The view was magnificent from the thirteenth floor. At one corner, I could see Pawar Public School, and on another, a twenty-one-floor-high building construction was going on in full swing. More than 120-degree-area in between was open.

This balcony had been my best investment ever. I spent hours sitting there, inhaling the fresh air, talking to pigeons. Sometimes I enjoyed looking at the school stadium right next door, which was always flooded with energetic kids. The clear sky and fresh air gave a hope for a better life. My evening tea with a smoke was a combination to die for!

'What is the plan now, author saab?'

'Hey, don't call me author saab. Let's find a suitable name.'

'Can I call you Arun ji?'

'No! You said you are my girlfriend... I mean, a friend. So you can call me Arun.'

'No, I cannot take your name.'

'Why?' She only shrugged in response.

'Can I call you sir?'

This time, I shrugged.

Later that evening, I was resting on my bed while Lalita lay down on the sofa. Her eyes were glued to her mobile phone. Her phone was getting notifications every minute. I guessed she was trying to hide the messages, but I could hear the buzz. I didn't ask anything upfront, assuming it was something personal. But it continued to vibrate and her facial expression worsened.

'Why do you look so tensed?'

'I am getting messages from my business partner.'

'Robin Hood?' She nodded in response. 'Oh! What is he saying?'

'That I should give him his money and that I cannot run from him.'

'You owe him money?'

'No no, he assumes I am making some big money with a super-rich client and he wants his share.'

'Is that bothering you?'

'Actually, he guessed that you were the one I ran away with.'

We looked at each and suddenly started laughing. After a few seconds of crazy laughter, she asked, 'What if they trap you in a false case?'

I smiled. 'Don't you worry.'

I picked up my cell phone and made a call.

'Hello, Inspector Vishal!'

12

As we grow older, going out to play with friends starts looking like a distant dream. Maybe because our environment changes; perhaps because our priorities shuffle. But in my life, this one man had always been there like a constant support – Vishal.

From a friend, he had taken on the role of a father for me, advising me like I was his own son. Born in the same city, Indore, we had studied together. He excelled in physical activities. He had won medals in sports, while I would sit in one corner and feel jealous of him.

Papa always had a big smile on seeing him. Initially I thought he was just being polite towards my father, but later found out that he was also a talebearer. Thanks to him, papa got to know everything that happened around me.

When I was in ninth standard, I sold off the silver *kada* I used to wear to buy a toy that could fly. I was mesmerized with the beauty of the toy and the science behind it. I told mom that I had got it as a gift from a friend. The fancy flying toy was enough to make me a hero in the friends' circle. Vishal came home one evening. An hour later, my father asked me where my kada was. At a loss for words, I looked at Vishal suspiciously. He shrugged, looking like the most innocent creature on earth.

When papa started shouting, the happiness on Vishal's face and anger on my father's created a cocktail of doubts in my head. Papa cleared all my confusion when he mercilessly took the toy from me and gave it to Vishal. When I saw the smile on his face widen, I wanted to smack him.

But all those things aside, when we grew up, he joined the Maharashtra Police as an inspector. I was fortunate to have him with me through the years. He wasn't just the contact that made sure all my work was done smoothly, but also my emergency financer. I often wondered how, despite a moderately good salary, his pocket never went out of cash. I am sure he was enjoying his income from other sources. Needless to say, I can't mention those sources here, otherwise he would kill me.

I walked into his office after I spoke to him over phone.

The police station walls were decaying and half the outer cement layer had already fallen off. Anyone who came to the station got a portion of the wall cement, either on their head or on their clothes. The tallest pinnacle of the station had bent like an ugly Leaning Tower of Pisa. The washroom was theoretically there, though no one used it. You'd need an oxygen mask to just enter the washroom. At one corner, there was a map of Maharashtra spread across the wall and the other wall displayed a framed picture of Mahatma Gandhi.

Half of the Lonavala police staff thought I was a journalist. Once Vishal had introduced me as a writer, and everyone had assumed the rest.

When I moved in through the rickety door, I saw Vishal sitting at his large desk. Hidden behind three enormous piles of files on his table, he barely had any space to work.

'How are you, author saab?' he said, busy scribbling something in Marathi, his handwriting looking more like ants crawling on the page.

He left his work and stood up to hug me, squishing me in his strong arms.

'Hey, Bhosle!' he screamed. 'Order two teas. One with less sugar for the author saab.'

Then, he turned towards me, asking, 'Would you please wait for a few minutes?'

I nodded and sat on the chair opposite to him. He was continuously shouting and screaming over a call. 'How could he run away to the Goa border?' He said the same thing thrice, almost roaring. 'I guess she has left Lonavala as the possibility of her being in Tarkali is high.' He went on and finally, the call ended some fifteen minutes later.

'What happened? All well?' I asked as the tea was served.

'Yeah! Usual work things.' He took a sip of his extra sugary tea and asked, 'Why don't you change your hairstyle? You put on too much oil.'

He always found some scope of improvement in me. Last time he had commented on my canvas shoes and before that, he had asked me to change my raincoat. So naturally, now I knew how to avoid all his *gyaan*.

'I came here to invite you for my Pune book launch.'

'Oh ! You have written another book? '

'Yes,' I said.

Great! Though I have only read the first one.'

'You are an asshole, but please come for the book launch.'

'I won't come yaar. Your book launches are boring.'

'Really?'

'Yeah! The only thing I like is the female turnout in your launches.' He winked.

I smiled at his lame joke. 'Please try to make it.'

'Bro, I am busy tracking a couple which is absconding from Mumbai. They stayed in Lonavala for a couple of days and have now shifted somewhere near Tarkali.'

'But why are you behind a couple?'

'The girl is the home secretary's relative.'

'Oh! Are they minors?'

'Are you digging out a thriller story from my case? I am sure we have better things to discuss.'

We changed the topic and started talking about things that had kept him busy, and also about his family. When two friends start talking, they tend to get lost in a world of their own.

'Arre yaar, I need your help,' I said as I handed over a box of rasgullas that I had brought from Kolkata.

'Finally you have proven that you have come here for money again,' Vishal said.

'How do you know that I need money?'

'Last time you came with Kakaji sweets and asked for twenty thousand rupees.'

'Oh man, listen!'

'No, I am not listening...'

I ignored his resistance. 'I had gone to Kolkata for the new book's launch.'

'I know! You posted so many pictures with Bengali girls.' He chuckled.

'Yes, and I met a girl whom I had hired for a massage.'

'What! Really? You hired a girl?' I nodded. 'Oh, fuck off, you *tharki* author.'

I narrated everything that had transpired as briefly as possible. I couldn't tell him everything, obviously, but he kept shouting in between. 'Are you serious?','This is not correct!','You are a moron' and other such things.

He settled down after thirty minutes of my one-sided narration. I made a goat face, ready for the last nail in the coffin. 'So, could you please help?'

'No!' His voice was sharp, clear and loud. 'I cannot help. You idiot, they may report to the police.'

'Hmm, but you *are* the police!'

'Yes... I am, but...'

'When I have my dear friend Vishal in the police, then no one can touch me.'

His face shone suddenly. He forgot that he was just an inspector. He left his chair and beamed like an immature *Singham*.

'I need your help in admitting Lalita to a rehabilitation centre.'

'Why don't you take Kajal's help?' he suggested. I went quiet and he made a sorry face in return.

'Sorry,' he muttered.

'You know very well that I haven't spoken to her even once in the last three years.'

He nodded.

I looked down and closed my eyes, memories of an awful past catching over. I almost flushed and said, 'Please don't pull her in any random conversation we have.'

He rubbed his chin and the frown on his face deepened as he said, 'There are a few good women rehabilitation centres in Pune.'

'Good!'

'Not really! There is a problem.' I raised my eyebrows and he explained, 'I cannot admit her to the women rehab. Before we can do that, we'd need to establish that we caught her in some raid or something of that sort, and there would be lots of paperwork required.'

'What is the problem in that? You can say that she was forced to work as a sex worker in Kolkata and we rescued her.'

'How do we explain that Lonavala police got her, and how did a prostitute land in Pune on her own?'

'Fuck off, Vishal!' I raised my voice. 'Call a fool a fool and an intelligent person intelligent, but always call a prostitute a lady.'

'You are shouting at me for that girl?'

He sat down and we both took a minute to calm down. A sense of concern had started appearing on my forehead. My palms were sweaty.

'Are you seriously thinking of removing her from the business of trafficking?' Vishal asked softly this time.

'Yes! And please don't use that word again,' I said politely.

'Hmm. Okay, let me explain some harsh realities to you.' He sounded hesitant with me for the first time, but continued, 'In a breakthrough data survey, four organizations working with trafficked women and sex workers have released a report which states that close to 77% women voluntarily return to sex work after they are rescued and sent to shelter homes.'

'Shit!' This couldn't be true. 'But why would they return to hell?'

'In most cases, a woman voluntarily takes up sex work, predominantly to escape poverty. After being rescued, they lose their source of income. This leaves their families impoverished, in addition to them being at the receiving end of social abuse and banter. The on-ground conditions are horrible.

'Look at what happened in Muzaffarnagar and Deoriya recently. At these rehab centres, there is no food to eat, and when there is some, it is not hygienic enough for consumption. There is no health care service for the inhabitants. And no support for HIV patients who require ART (antiretroviral therapy). Even if that is provided, it is with the stigma that all sex workers are HIV infected.'

'Oh, this is hell.' I groaned.

'You have no idea how a woman is treated in the so-called sex market.'

'I am not interested in the problem,' I said, feeling disappointed.

'How will you find the solution if you are not interested in the problem?' He always does that.

'I want her to study further and do something meaningful with her life.'

'Why are you interested in her life?'

'Because...' I started sharing my thoughts, but then I realized that he already had so many negative ideas in his mind regarding this whole episode. 'That's something personal, Vishal.'

'Keep your reasons to yourself if it is so personal. Listen, I have to leave for Goa for a case and it will take some time.'

'Oh! I can't delay this more, so what would you suggest?'

'Mumbai has better women rehabilitation centres, but I need to find some contacts. Plus, I'd need to work on the documents. Does she have any ID card?'

'Yes, she has an Aadhaar card.'

'Share a copy of that on WhatsApp.'

'Where am I going to keep her till all this is sorted?'

'You can book a hotel for her or something.'

'I don't have that kind of money yaar.'

'Then there is only one option.'

'What's that?'

He winked and said, 'She will stay with you.'

13

When I reached home, Lalita was sleeping on the sofa. I had a spare set of house keys which I had used. The image of a girl sleeping on the sofa brought back some old memories. I wondered if she could have slept on the comfortable bed if I wasn't there.

Her face was serene, and she looked like any other girl. You couldn't guess by looking at her face that she had gone through so much. All that was hard to even imagine for us and yet, she had lived that harsh life with enormous courage and there were many more who were still stuck in that human-made hell hole.

I strolled into the balcony and sat on the plastic chair. I spent some time smoking, alongside checking notifications on Facebook and Instagram. I saw a few beautiful pictures, which made it seem like every girl was smiling and every boy was rich. We are so happy on Facebook and Instagram; pain exists only in real life.

I tried hard to reply to every message that had come in. Some messages simply amused me.

Can you please give me an author-signed copy? I am a student, and I don't have money to buy the book.

I replied, *Pls study hard and earn enough so that you don't have to ask anyone for freebies.*

Even on WhatsApp, there were about twenty unread messages. One of them was a very important one.

Hi Mr Arun, I am a film rights agent working for a major film production house and we are interested in purchasing the film rights for your book. We have e-mailed you the details of the offer, the amount we can offer and the terms & conditions involved.

I had just finished reading the message when I guess the sender saw me online and messaged instantly, *Can we connect over a call in another half an hour?*

I didn't reply, and instead started searching for news around women's shelters in India. To my horror, I saw some scary headlines.

A prostitution racket scam had been leaked in a women's shelter in Gujarat and many politicians seemed to be involved in it. I clicked on a few more links and found a headline: *The pathetic condition of women's shelter homes.*

It had a series of images which made it hard to believe that people lived there. Worry ran through my mind and I closed the google search and checked the Instagram notifications again. I guess I was addicted to social media.

'Hi sir!' Lalita's voice came from beside me.

I looked at her, and noticed she looked nice in my baggy T-shirt and shorts.

'When did you come from Lonavala?' she asked.

'While you were sleeping.'

'What happened? You look worried.'

'Nothing! Just got a random film rights offer,' I lied.

'What is a film right?'

A smile came onto my face. 'Actually, honestly, I am wondering what I'd say about you.' She looked confused. 'If someone asks how you are related to me, how should I introduce you?'

'How about... as your girlfriend?' she suggested.

'No no, that is not a good idea. I have relatives and a big fan base in the city. It would complicate things unnecessarily.'

There was silence for a few seconds and the heavenly balcony view was the only saving grace.

The piercing ringtone of my phone took my eyes to the film agent's contact flashing on my phone screen. I ignored the call, clearly not in the mood for this conversation.

He called again. I was about to blast at him, but just then, an idea sneaked into my head.

'Hey, Lalita!' She looked at me attentively. 'Can you take this call and tell the guy that sir is not here? No, wait! Say, sir is busy and will call later.'

I didn't even wait for her agreement and picked the call on speaker.

Lalita said in her signature Hindi blended in Bangla, 'Hello, who is this?'

'Can I talk to Mr Arun Kumar? I am Naveen from Film Media production.'

'Sir is in a business meeting right now.'

'Oh! With whom? I mean, can you tell me if he is meeting any production house?'

I nodded and Lalita said, 'Yes.'

'Oh!' There was silence for a few seconds.

'Thank you, ma'am. May I know with whom I am speaking?'

'Lalita.'

'Are you his...,' he probed, '...manager?'

I nodded and she replied with a 'Yes!'

The call ended, soon after which I got an email from him.

Hi Arun sir,

I had a word with your manager and got to know that you are in touch with another production house. We were willing to reconsider the proposal that was offered to you. We seriously feel we can revise the film rights price.

Regards,
Naveen

I read that message again and smiled, while Lalita stood there, quite confused.

I told her confidently, 'If anyone asks you, just say you are author Arun Kumar's manager.'

I was a little tired and wondered what to cook for dinner. I made the chapattis and Lalita tried her hand at making some sort of curry. She had enquired about my favourite food and raised her concern that we had run out of spices in the kitchen. We had our dinner in silence and I cherished the feeling of not having to eat alone.

I went to sleep early while Lalita was busy with her cell phone on the sofa. I understood she would not be sleeping early.

I woke up at around midnight. I realized that unlike my usual routine, I had forgotten to switch off the phone internet. So when I picked up my phone, it had seven good night messages with beautiful hearts and some kissing emojis, and a few complains like - *Why are you ignoring me, sir? Why are you not replying to me?*

I kept the phone on silent mode and noticed that Lalita was looking at me.

'What happened? Not sleepy yet?' I asked her

'No sir! How can my body clock change in a day?' she flashed a sad smile, or I can say, a fake smile.

I understood what she was hinting at. I lifted my head and rested on my angular hand, still snuggling under the quilt and asked, 'So now that you are appointed as my manager, do you know what you're supposed to do?'

'No! I guess I need to talk to people and arrange *dhanda* or business for you?' She was explaining the profile of a pimp to me.

I flared my nostrils but answered politely, 'Yes, but that is not entirely true. Let me guide you on what to do.'

I sat on the bed and she sat on the sofa, almost a couple of metres apart. The late-night silence was saving me the effort of having to talk loudly. 'You need to reply to my Facebook, Twitter and Instagram messages, as well as phone calls.'

There was excitement on her face. It seemed she liked her new work profile. 'But most of the things would be in English.' She whined.

'Try your best! Let's see what you can read and understand?'

She nodded before asking, 'Any more tips?'

'There are three things you should remember –Don't reply for me. Always say, I will discuss it with sir and get back to you. Second, sir is very busy and let me check with him. If you fail to understand what they want, just give my card and say write an email to sir.'

She lost the excitement and the curve of her lips fell downwards.

'What's the worry?'

'Do you think I'm ready?'

'You are more than ready.'

'I'm not confident.'

'Don't worry. It's only for a month or so.'

'Why only for one month?'

'I will help you shift to a women rehabilitation centre after that.'

She went silent. I could see disappointment on her face clearly, even in the dim light. I faked a yawn and she slid on the sofa, peeping into her cell phone again.

It's hard to sleep when your heart is at war with your mind. I thought of asking something related to her mother or about her past life. Her traumatic past would make her realize the worth of the current situation, I felt.

'Hey Lalita! You never tried to find a different job, after you became free?'

'I am not that educated and smart.'

The lump in my throat was making it hard for me to speak. I rubbed my eyes with my left palm. 'Hey, can I ask you something?'

She nodded while sitting up again. 'You have had pretty diverse life experiences. If you are comfortable, share something nice. Perhaps some interesting meeting with a good guy?'

'I had a very weird encounter once.'

'Share only if it is good.'

'Good or bad, you can decide for yourself.'

14

In Lalita's own words

My mom was shifted to a private hospital. I had borrowed some money from Rani for her treatment. In return, she took a promise from me that I must work double my capacity. I used to entertain three or four customers in a day. I had arranged half of the amount which was required for my mother's treatment by working overtime. I wanted to live for my mom, to give her life, even at the cost of dying from within every day.

I still remember the day when I had managed to gather a decent amount for mom's treatment. I called her to give her the good news, but mamaji picked up. I asked about mom and how she had been, to which mamaji replied in a sorrowful tone.

'Lalita, money is not required now beti. We have lost the battle.'

The only reason why I was living was now gone. My mother was no more. There was nothing left for me in this world of desperate men. It was hard to keep count of how many people I had slept with by that time. Each one of them had offered me a tip, sometimes a small amount, while other times, it was close to five hundred to a thousand rupees, which was mine to keep.

Gathering all that money, I was set free one year later. I had paid all the debt and cleared Rani's dues. The sense of freedom was alien to me, so I went shopping to cheer myself up. I bought all the expensive brands of clothing that I had always craved for. I walked into a cosmetics-shop and purchased my favourite things, along with expensive perfumes. I checked my cart which was full of all kinds of fancy items. The shopkeeper treated me with utmost respect and that's how I realized what it meant to be wealthy. Wealth is not about having a lot of money; it's about having a lot of options and respect.

Soon, I shifted to a bigger brothel which had many girls. There, I got in touch with Mallika. I did not know whether that was her real name or not, but we both were special escorts. We were reserved for five-star hotel customers only. Naturally, we got acquainted with a lot of these five-star hotel staff people too. I had seen the other side of many politicians, doctors and well-known businessmen by then.

Mallika was from Bangladesh and she was the only one with whom I could talk sincerely. The government had passed the new controversial Indian citizenship law and rumour mills were teeming with new agendas every day. The media was flooded with news around Hindu and Muslim protests.

On a Saturday, protesters blocked motorways and attacked trains and stations in Kolkata. I was getting worried about my only true friend.

'Hey Mallika, what is your religion?' My curiosity about her religion increased when I learned that she was from Bangladesh.

'Do prostitutes have a religion?'

We smiled. Probably, a brothel was one of the rare places which was secular. A place where everyone was treated rationally, irrespective of any religious politics, based on the amount of cash they could generate.

It was Navratri time and Kolkata was decked up like a bride. Dashami marked the end of Durga Puja, where everyone gathered to bid adieu to the goddess. Women donned the traditional red and white saree to apply sindoor to the goddess. I too wore the same saree and looked at myself in the mirror a little too long.

'You are living in your dreams,' Mallika said.

'Why?'

'This saree and the celebration is only for married ladies.'

'So? One day I will also get married,' I said with a smile.

She laughed, and I hated her for it. 'Who would marry a prostitute?'

'I am sure there would be someone.'

'There is a difference between sympathy and love.'

'Sympathy is also a form of love, I feel,' I told her the same thing that I had once said to my mom and the irony of the situation hit me.

'Sympathy is temporary. It will become a burden after some time. Only love can last long.'

'One day, I would be loved by someone.'

There was a raid at the brothel a few days later and everything was seized. Mallika and I had to spend the night at the police station. We had to sacrifice almost all our cash to buy back our freedom.

The brothel owner was asked to close the business. We had only two options left – we could work in an open brothel like Sonagachi, or we could work at a massage parlour.

So we started working at a spa. We barely made any money, despite spending all our energy and rubbing the bodies of the big, fat, sleazy customers. That industry had a good number of people from the Northeast. Most of them treated us as local competition and made our work tougher. Even customers preferred them over us and we ended up feeling like second-class citizens there.

Hard luck hit us again when there was a raid at the massage parlour too. We had to stay in the police station again and a lot of cash was demanded against our release. But, the police inspector was not satiated with just the cash. He walked towards us slowly. I shivered in fear, but Mallika was staring right at him. He diverted his attention and turned to Mallika and said, 'I am tired.'

I did not understand what he meant, but Mallika was experienced and smarter. She said, 'Do you need a body massage, sir?'

That night, Mallika worked hard for our release.

Once we got out, we were sure that India was not a safe place for such a business. Upon talking to others in the trade, we discovered another option.

We were offered a bar-dancer profile in Pattaya, Thailand. We were thrilled at the prospect of going abroad, but the passport application got rejected because of the unavailability of proper address proofs and other documents.

I had seen enough struggles by the age of twenty-two. Two years of being in this filthy industry, I had started to believe that even dirt was cleaner than me.

I had encountered almost all kinds of men in life by then. And just when I was losing all hope, a bizarre thing happened.

I was called to The Park hotel for a businessman who was seeking my services. He earnestly welcomed me into his room and I was apprehensive if he was going to do anything at all. For a man in his early thirties, he was rather average looking. He must have been a rich man, staying in such a fancy place. He introduced himself as Vijai.

'Lalita ji, please sit,' he said as soon as I entered his room.

He offered me a seat on the plush sofa. Honestly, nobody had given me such respect before until now. He dug into the wardrobe and pulled out a red T-shirt and pink pyjamas.

'Could you please wear this for me?' he asked politely.

I nodded.

It was not a new request. As in, a lot of customers asked me to wear their favourite dresses. I went to the washroom and changed from my tight-fitted red halter dress to the comfortable T-shirt and pyjamas. It was a little loose for me and the mirror said that I was not looking glamorous at all.

I came out and looked at him. His dark eyes were red, and he stared at me and the T-shirt that I was wearing.

'Let's go out for dinner,' he said with a poker face.

We went out and he ordered my favourite food, asking questions about my life. My answers were short and to the point.

'What you do, sir?' I asked out of curiosity.

He did not share much, just told me that he worked in a college in Delhi.

We finished dinner and he ordered some dessert, without asking me.

I ate the soft rasgullas and he kept looking at me, a permanent smile pasted on his face. I offered some to him, but he politely denied. We returned to the room and he was sitting and gaping at me. I wondered when he would start the action. I was already stuffed with a lot of food.

He tried to talk about a lot of varied things, and all I could gather was that he wished to talk to someone. We talked for hours, not knowing how time went by. For the first time, someone heard me out so patiently.

Around 2 a.m., I asked him, 'Are you not sleepy, sir?'

He nodded and said, 'Let's sleep.'

He moved towards the bed and whispered, 'Could you please remove your clothes?'

'Of course!'

I stood there in my undergarments and he signalled me to the bed. I neared him and gave him a soft hug.

'Can you please switch the lights off?' he requested.

I did that, but there was a night lamp glowing and he asked me to switch that off too.

We both got into the soft and cosy blanket. He hugged me softly and slid the only layer of clothing away. Now my breast touched his chest, his heart hammering.

He put his finger inside the lining of my underwear. On cue, I started sliding it down, but he stopped me. Instead, he hugged me tight.

His voice was soft when he said, 'How are you, Astha?'

Was he hallucinating? Was I imagining this?

'Could you please caress my back and call me by my name?'

'Oh, Vijai! Anything for you, dear.'

I ran my nails lightly along his bare back and faked a moan.

'Vijai, you are too good.'

'How are you, my love?'

Let me confess,I was quite turned on and tried kissing him.

He refused to kiss me, and I continued to snuggle him. He kept calling me Astha. We did not realize when we slept like that.

I woke up in the early hours next morning and got ready to leave. Vijai was also up and offered me a tip of five hundred rupees. I was curious to know what was happening.

'If I may ask, who is Astha, sir?'

'Astha is my wife.'

'Oh! Where is she?'

He puckered his lips and diverted his gaze before replying, "She is no more."

15

I ordered a copy of the Bengali version of *Rapidex English Speaking Course* for Lalita. I had spent the last fifteen minutes lecturing Lalita on how to improve her English and how it could help her. She accepted my words, but with the reluctance of a student who always wondered why the subject even existed. English was just a language for her, but it was a means of survival for an author.

'Are you ready?'

'Almost...' she said looking at the list.

I bought her a new SIM card and logged into my Twitter and Facebook accounts from her phone. I coached her a little about what she could say to reply and how. She started checking my social media messages.

She had landed in Pune under special circumstances and needed to shop for many things. So I suggested going out shopping.

She was taking a long time to get ready, even when she did not have any fancy clothes to deck herself up in. I was getting impatient, as it had been years that I had waited for a woman to dress up. Lalita came out of the washroom in track pants and a T-shirt. I smiled. It's amazing to see your clothes worn by a beautiful lady. Gone were the traces of Lalita that I had seen the first time. Today, with no makeup and her hair tied back neatly in a ponytail, she looked like a different girl altogether.

'The list is ready, sir,' Lalita said, handing me a sheet of paper.

I stared at those scribbles in Bengali and looked at her with a blank face. I raised my eyebrows. The text looked as if it was written by someone who had tried to blend Hindi with English and Bangla, and had finally produced something entirely different in the process.

'Could you please read out the list in Hindi?' I said.

She took the list from me and started reading the contents out loud. 'Toothbrush, slippers, shoes, two shirts, T-shirts, nail polish, shorts, facial cream, towel...' I smiled on recollecting some old memories.

'That's all?'

'No, two more things.'

'Tell me!'

She hesitated a bit before saying, 'I have only one bra...'

'Oh sure!' I gritted my teeth and added underwear and sanitary pads to the list.

We went to Pune Central mall. She was amazed to see the decoration at the entrance. We went to a medium-ranged family clothing store and picked up the essentials listed by her. It felt like we had been shopping for several hours, but my watch said it had been an hour only.

I still hated shopping, but watching Lalita and her smile made me realize that she was still a little girl, after all. Finally, I paid the bill, and we went to the top floor. The food court was brimming with the aroma of various delicacies and temptations. We ordered a medium cheese burst pizza and took a corner table, viewing the city from the top floor.

'Have we got everything?'

She simply nodded her head while taking a sip of her drink. Her silence said she had been thinking about something. After a while, she broke the silence and asked, 'Why do you like me so much?'

'Excuse me?'

'Why buy all this for me when I will leave the place in a month anyway?'

I looked away and took a long sip of my cold drink. I took a few seconds to reply, 'Because you are my manager.'

'Really?' She rolled her eyes.

'Yes, and a great author like me cannot afford to have a poor manager.'

We both laughed.

It was a usual evening and I had just come back from a friend's place. I was pleasantly surprised to find the house smelling of good food. Lalita had made dal. My attention then went to the chapattis. Her rare art on chapattis made it look like a rounded Sri Lankan map. But the improvement in the chapatti-making had been substantial.

She served the dinner with affection.

'It is delicious,' I said after taking the first bite.

'You said the same thing when I cooked for the first time.' She chuckled.

'Today, it is more delicious.'

'Thanks.'

I was enjoying my food and the free luxury I was getting for now. My kitchen had transformed owing to Lalita's magic. All the bottles had proper caps now and were aligned in a row. The bigger ones were arranged behind the smaller ones. I realized I had three containers for salt and two for sugar. Surprisingly, I also noticed that my kitchen rack was spacious enough to accommodate a lot more. No containers were leaking, leaving oil marks on shelves. The drainage was also clean.

I wondered how the house would look after she was gone.

Once we finished dinner, she started arranging her bed on the sofa. I had a few couches and she had moved them together to make a more comfortable sleeping place.

I had started reducing my conversations with Lalita, because I wanted to avoid any emotional bonding with her. The mind knows the truth, but it is tough to convince the heart that beats every second.

I posted some motivational lines on Facebook and got busy replying to messages and checking the notifications. After a while, I switched the internet off on the phone, getting ready to sleep. The girl on the sofa was looking at me, her big Bengali eyes glittering in the dim light.

I closed my eyes and tried to sleep. That's when a thought occurred to me – I have one lakh followers to chat with, but she has only one. Me. I rubbed my palms and ran them over my face and said, 'Hey, why are you still up?'

'I am not sleepy yet.'

'Why so?'

'I have spent years doing the night shift,' she said in a low voice.

I stretched my arm and switched on the night lamp on the bedside. I sat back up and faced her. She also got up and sat on the couch.

'How are you managing the Twitter and Facebook replies?' I asked to divert attention.

'I am usually sending only three kinds of messages – one with smiling emojis; second saying stay in touch and last saying take care.'

I had noticed that I had less unread messages. After the initial stress of why the sudden slowdown, I had realised that my manager had started off with the work.

'Do you understand the queries and messages?'

'Not exactly... not all the time actually.'

I guessed I had given the wrong task to her.

'Okay, listen! Tomorrow is the Pune launch of the book, and there will be a lot of people from the media and all. Remember, if anyone asks you, how many copies of my books have been sold, just say a million copies roughly.'

'Wow! That's a lot!' As an afterthought, she asked, 'How much has it actually sold?'

'Not even half of that.'

'Oh! Why give out the wrong information then?'

'Don't worry about that. Almost every artist, painter, designer, author and others in the creative field doesn't earn much. They just lead a fancy life. Look at me!' I said shrugging and looking around the small place.

'I get it. But then, if it is the same for everyone, why exhibit such false prosperity?'

'If you are rich and famous, people will believe in you. Everyone wants to hear success stories.'

'But failures have far better lessons to teach,' she said, looking confused.

'Who wants lessons? We all are tirelessly slogging to achieve an illusion of perfection.'

She was not so taken aback by this. 'Seems like success is a pretension everywhere.'

'Yes! Everyone is struggling in the real world, but doing excellent on Facebook or Instagram.'

She went silent now. I fathomed that I had given her more reasons to not sleep.

'What do you wish to achieve in life? Your dream?' I asked to get talking again.

'I never thought about it.'

'A little girl with a dream today becomes a successful woman tomorrow.'

'I don't have any dreams.'

'Hmm. Maybe just think about what will make you happy the most. That could be a dream, you know. It doesn't take so much thought. Try!' I coaxed.

'Okay. I think I have a dream then.'

'That was quick!' I smiled. 'What is that?'

'I want to have a loving husband.'

'Why do you need a husband?'

'Because... You know...' she tried to answer but stopped midway, and then simply said, 'I don't know.'

It felt like someone had asked about her secret boyfriend. 'I guess you miss having a family. Is that so?'

'Maybe... But like you said, a dream is an illusion.'

Every single time I had tried to make her happy, I had ended up making her feel dejected.

'You are an author, you have written so many stories. Why don't you tell me a story?'

'No! I want you to be educated enough to read my books on your own.'

'These?' She pointed at the book shelf.

I nodded.

'These are in English!'

I was about to laugh.

'Can I ask a personal question?' she asked and I nodded my head.

'How old are you? Actually thirty-eight or is that also a fake number for others?'

'Thirty-eight!'

'You never thought of marrying?'

This wasn't a conversation I wanted to have. So, I extended my arm to switch off the night lamp. 'I think we should sleep.'

'But you did not answer my question?'

'I am happy on Facebook and Instagram. Why do I need a wife?'

'Hmm. Everyone is struggling in the real world and doing excellent on Facebook or Instagram,' she mumbled.

16

Hi Vishal! Today is the book launch. I dropped my only friend an invitation message.

Thanks for the reminder. I will be there. He replied almost instantly.

I called up all my media contacts, inviting them to cover the event. Anything on home grounds was comparatively stress-free to manage. The anchor, décor, seating and store arrangements were easily taken care of, with just a few phone calls.

I settled Lalita on the living room sofa and passed on some pointers. I guided her about when she had to take the gifts or flowers from my hand and when she had to pretend to take notes.

She heard me and asked, 'Can I take notes in Bangla?'

I rolled my eyes and speculated if she had understood any of my instructions. That had a lot of English words thrown in it.

'You may need to take down some phone numbers. Please carry a pen and a diary, even if there is nothing to write. You need to pretend that you are writing something.'

She nodded. 'Can I pretend to write something in Bangla?'

I closed my fist, my eyes now slits.

'Get ready. We need to head out for the launch soon.' I closed the discussion.

She took close to half an hour to get ready. When she came out, she looked great in a beautiful fitted dress that we had bought the other day. She was a pretty girl and as she transitioned into a normal life routine, her face had started to look more serene and calm. She had put on some makeup after a long time. Her lipstick looked a bit too shiny to me, but it looked good on her nonetheless.

My mind played on loop the thought that the world would be jealous of me today.

We sat in the car and I directed the driver towards the Crossword book store where the launch was planned.

On our way, I asked Lalita casually, 'Listen, how many copies have I sold till now?'

'I know you have sold more than a minion.'

'Not minion, it's million.'

She nodded and said, 'Same.'

There was a big question mark on my face when she asked something to further puncture my smile. 'How many zeros are there in million?' I was totally out of words.

We had reached the launch venue a few minutes before the assigned time. I received a warm welcome from the store manager and staff. I called up Vishal when we were about to reach. He was late, as usual. I wanted him to unveil the book at the event today. After all, he was the only person in this city I loved dearly.

The emcee came to me and whispered, 'Sir, can we start with the launch? Readers are waiting for you.'

I nodded and went up on the stage. I looked around at more than sixty readers who were waiting for me.

They saw me smiling and waving at them, and the book store reverberated with applause. The affection and respect that

I received that day was something each author lives and strives to achieve, even if they did not have any money. There were a few unknown faces amidst the regular ones, who had attended some launches earlier as well. Then, my eyes landed on the young Bengali girl, Lalita. She was standing in one corner, engulfed in silence and hushed emotions.

I signalled at Lalita to come on the stage. She walked up confidently. There was applause again as I guided her towards the books wrapped in shiny paper. She launched my eighth book with a dazzling smile and media people clicked several pictures. Just then, an idiot walked into the event in police uniform. I made a face and Vishal understood that he was late.

Right behind him, *she* made an entry. I went blank. I looked at Lalita and a strange sensation ran through me. I asked myself, 'Why and how did *she* land up here? Did she come with Vishal?' My attention was drawn back to the stage with the anchor's voice echoing in the mic.

The same old introduction was made, and I gave my usual speech that I had delivered in Kolkata too. I continued the marathon of this one-sided English monologue. I saw someone in the audience yawning, and then two more. I understood that any more words from me will make them collapse with boredom.

'Let's have an open house now. You can ask away your questions,' I said ending my monologue.

'Sir, we are from *Sakal* Pune, a Marathi daily. Could you give us an interview?'

I nodded and signalled at my manager. She came running and I said, 'Could you please take down their contact so we can have an interview after the launch.'

The press was thrilled with the presence of a manager. After all, it was the first time I had acted like a celebrity.

My attention was continuously shifting to the unwanted lady; her presence had upset me a great deal. She left after a few minutes. Vishal came and wished me good luck for the book and picked one copy, asking me to sign it. It was amazing to sign a book for such a dear friend. He had to leave soon after because of work commitment.

I heaved a sigh of relief and stretched a little more on the sofa. I felt tranquil when I was sure that she had left. I got busy talking to my readers.

A teenager came forward and asked over-enthusiastically, 'Sir, can I ask you something, personal?'

I gulped in anticipation. I knew when people sought permission to ask a personal question, they were mostly unnerving. Even without waiting for my permission, she asked, 'How are you related to Lalita ma'am?'

'She is my manager.'

She blushed like a watermelon. I pretended that I was in a hurry and got down from the stage.

My eyes landed on the *Pune Mirror's* journalist. He was eyeing me keenly.

The silly teenager girl blurted, 'Sir, you both look great. A perfect couple.'

17

To my delight, two newspapers had covered the book launch the next day. But the happiness lasted only till I read the coverage.

Who says authors do not earn?

Meet popular author Arun Kumar, his PR Manager claims he sells close to one lakh copies of every book and that he charges a hefty fee as a college speaker. The author is an inspiration for many.

I almost screamed, 'What! Who told them all this?'

The second newspaper had beaten the scope of my imagination.

Has the author found a new partner?

They had printed a picture from the book launch event where Lalita and I stood on the stage, proudly exhibiting the book. Lalita was smiling like the happiest girl on earth.

Author Arun Kumar was seen with his new girlfriend at his book launch event. She also launched his latest book. The new-generation love knows no boundaries, even when the partner is fifteen years older and a well-known author. It is a matter of personal choice and we respect the author for his work.

Then, they had mentioned a few lines around my book, in the passing.

I read the article twice and flushed, 'People know more stuff about my life than I do myself.'

Lalita saw the articles too, and her lips curved up into a smile.

'Are you happy?'

'I have never seen my picture in a newspaper,' she said joyously

'Do you have any idea about what they have written?'

She shook her head with a silly smile pasted on her lips. Somebody's pain was someone else's reason for celebration. I looked away and opened Instagram to distract myself. It had ten unread messages, sadly all on the same lines. One user had sent multiple messages.

Sir, can I ask you a personal question?

Are you dating Lalita ma'am?

Are you married to Lalita ma'am?

I sulked internally while Lalita was lost in her own world of illusions. There was a knock on the door. A sudden chill ran through my body. I usually never get any visitors.

I instructed Lalita to go into the kitchen as I went to open the door. I didn't want to support the running rumours. Unlike any other average Indian, I was relaxed on seeing a man in police uniform.

'Vishal! How are you, bro?'

'I'm fine yaar.'

'Come inside!'

He walked in with a look of amazement and appreciation. He didn't need my permission to walk in like that. He roamed about, taking in each nook of the house.

'Wow, your house looks so clean and organised now.'

I thanked him with a smile.That's when he bent and picked the newspapers sitting proudly on the sofa. 'Wah, writer saab! Big man, media and photoshoot.'

I pulled a couple of chairs into the balcony. He walked in, lighting a cigarette.

'Sir!' Lalita called out. She was standing with two glasses of water. He took the glass of water and glanced at her unblinking.

'Namaste sir!' She was shivering in fear. I could see how much the police scared her. I nudged him.

'Can you make some tea for us all?' I asked Lalita I diverted Vishal's attention to me as she left. 'Hey, why are you staring at her like that?'

'I was doing my investigation.'

'Are you at a crime scene?'

He suddenly became serious. 'Who told you to bring Lalita to the book launch?'

'Why? What is the problem?'

'What is the problem? Are you insane?' I shrugged. 'You made her public and now everyone knows her name.'

'So?'

'How would I arrange her stay in a women's rehabilitation shelter now? What would I say if someone asks about her?'

Oh shit! My apprehensions shone on my forehead.

While I was still brooding, he added, 'I have an alternative solution for you.'

'Solution?' I liked the hopeful tone after all the negative talk.

'Why can't she work as a full-time caretaker in some wealthy family?'

'Fuck you!' I said clear and loud, 'No.'

'But why?'

'I don't know why, but I don't want that.'

'Why?'

I refused to give him a reply. 'Because you love a prostitute, don't you?' he said.

'Shut up!' I almost shouted.

'Sorry, I should not be using that word.'

'Please never address her like that.'

'Fine! But the fact remains that you love her, Arun.'

'That's not true.'

He understood that direct investigation will not work and tried another way. 'Just cut short your explanation and answer in a yes or no,' he began his police-style interrogation.

'Do you like her?' Vishal asked again, and sternly this time.

'Yes.'

'Are you attracted to her?'

'I don't know'.

'Only yes or no, please.'

'Yes.'

'Do you love her? Be honest!'

'Yes.'

'Do you want to marry her?'

'No.'

'Why don't you want to marry her?'

'Because I am already married.'

18

In Lalita's own words

I had been staring at my picture in the newspaper the whole day. It was beyond my wildest dream. No one in my entire village had ever appeared in a newspaper. I cut that portion of the paper and kept it with me.

I should confess that I had started liking Arun sir even more now. He treated me like family and respected me. When he called me on stage for the book launch, I was overwhelmed. Everyone was clapping for me, showing their respect. But sometimes, I feel that he deliberately conceals his feelings from me. Unlike so many times in my life, he is the one man I have longed to touch. He, on the other hand, has never ever tried to do that. He maintains a distance from me. We were two different souls and two different bodies which were always apart in a single room.

Honestly, when I got to know him, I got the impression that he was a rich man. I was pleased about my luck, but found out soon that he was a celebrity on social media, and a common man in real life. His small rented flat had the basic necessities, but that's about it.

The central wall of the room had a big golden steel frame that had caught my attention when I had stepped into the house the first time. Young Arun sir's picture stood smiling confidently in the frame. I guessed there was some story behind the frame. But one thing I knew very well – even though he had a small house, he had a big heart.

My heart had cried when he told me that he'd be sending me to a rehabilitation centre.

When we went shopping, he recommended clothes for me. I understood he was a novice in shopping for women, but I still bought whatever he suggested. Perhaps he wants to see me in those dresses, I thought. But still, I checked the price tag before buying anything. I didn't want to take advantage of his feelings.

He was pretending to look elsewhere when I was picking undergarments and sanitary pads. I smiled at his innocence. For me, shame and hesitation were just superficial concepts.

I asked him several times whether he's married or not, but he avoided the question. But there was surely something hidden within him. Why was he living alone? I often wondered why he spent so much time in the balcony.

He painstakingly trained me in basic etiquettes. I loved his instructions and authority over me. After all, there was someone who had not lost hope in me. I realized in the process that his writing world and stardom were all fake. He wears the hat of a very common man but roams in India like a bestselling author.

I started managing his social media, especially Facebook. He got a few 'good morning' and too many 'good night' messages. I mostly replied with 'Thank you' or 'Ok', using more emojis. I avoided all the silly messages of some readers who wanted to be personal with him.

Once, when he found out that I was intentionally ignoring some such messages, he was angry. He even shouted at me.

'Why this negligence, Lalita? You have to reply to everyone.'

'They have bad intentions,' I tried to explain.

'What intentions?'

'They wanted to flirt or be involved with you?'

'And how do you know that?'

'Because I am a girl.'

He smiled and then laughed loudly. 'I have not met 99% of these people with whom I chat. They don't know me, but still, they love me. They know my work, they love the author in me, not my personal self.'

I frowned at his logic.

'My readers deserve a basic reply, because they have made me who I am today.'

I did not understand his long and over-emotional speech, but I concluded that I needed to say what he wanted to hear.

I went to his book launch with mixed feelings. I had never been to any book launch before. People in the audience were very average looking; most of them looked very studious. I had gone there more for a formality, but was thrilled when a reader came and asked for a selfie. I smiled at the respect and importance that was displayed to me. I was standing near a journalist who was clicking pictures.

A few media people came and asked me something, which I did not understand completely. What could I do! I nodded to whatever they asked. Unexpectedly, when a middle-aged lady walked to the book launch, Arun sir's behaviour changed. He got fidgety.

When Arun sir was busy signing copies for readers, the strange lady came to me.

'Hi, I am Kajal.'

'Lalita.'

'So, how are you related to the author?' she asked.

I frowned and did not know what to say.

'I represent a publisher and we want him to write for us. That's why I am asking,' she explained.

'I'm his manager and you can call him at this number.' I handed sir's visiting card.

'We wish to send him some documents, so we would need his address.'

I started telling her the address, but she suddenly stopped me.

'This is the author's address. He is a big author and might be travelling to different places. Please share your address, Lalita.'

'It's the same address,' I replied.

Her eyes suddenly grew bigger as she raised her eyebrows asking me, 'You stay with him?'

19

My WhatsApp was flooded with queries about Lalita. I was not in a mood to chat and switched off the internet. I went for a long walk, by myself. When I came back home, I noticed that Lalita had cleaned the house and was busy cooking.

I changed into comfortable clothes and noticed the delicious-looking dal, *aloo ki sabzi* and chapattis neatly placed on the table. She had tried her hands at chapattis for the third time. The shape and size of the chapatti indicated that she was a good learner.

I dipped a bite of the chapatti into the lip-smacking curry. And just as the bite landed in my mouth, I couldn't swallow it. She was looking at me intently. I understood what I needed to do.

'The food is awesome.'

She beamed with happiness. Under her watchful gaze, I finished two chapattis with great difficulty.

'How is your English training going?'

'Good, I am working hard. I have seen a few videos on YouTube also.'

'Did you learn any new words?'

'Oh yes! Frustration and depression.'

I looked at her and wondered what kind of videos she had been watching.

'If that's what the videos have taught you, maybe use the books more.'

She nodded, without another word. I could sense an awkward silence in the air today.

'Listen, don't cook anything in the evening. We will go out for dinner.'

She cheered up and we cleared the table.

I thought of taking a power nap and saw her preparing her bed on the sofa alongside.

'Can I ask you something?' Lalita asked.

'Yes, please.'

'You did not like the food na?'

'No no. It was delicious. It's my birthday today, so I decided to have dinner outside.'

'Really?' her big eyes became even wider.

I nodded.

'Happy birthday, sir! Why didn't you tell me before? I could have cooked something special.'

I thanked myself internally for hiding my birthday for this exact reason. 'You already did. Thank you.' Although I wanted to say that she was not here to cook and clean.

'How do you normally celebrate your birthday?'

I tried to recollect my previous birthdays, realizing painfully that I had spent quite a few without any celebration. I always felt my birthdays were the happiest when they were spent on Instagram and Facebook, replying to my readers. My attention diverted to the large frame on the wall. I looked at my smiling picture. I recollected the childhood memories around the best birthday when I had received this frame as a gift. Lalita was sitting close to that frame.

'Can you please pass that large frame?' I asked her.

She handed over the same with a poker face. I brushed my hand over my picture fondly. The smiling photo was taken when I was thirty years old.

Lalita was looking at me like I had lost my mind.

'On every birthday, my father gifted me something that belonged to him. He had given me this frame on one of my birthdays.'

'But it looks pretty old,' she observed correctly. There was something more to the story, but I did not feel the need to elaborate. 'What kind of restaurant do you want to go to?'

Right then, before she could reply, she got a call from an unknown number. She took the call and kept saying 'yes' intermittently. Then, the call got disconnected.

'A lady wants to come and meet you and was enquiring about you?'

'Which lady?'

'She was a publisher, reporter or something...'

I started getting restless and perhaps it showed.

'You should be happy that someone is coming to talk to...'

'But no one knows my home address. What did she ask?'

'She asked if you are home and I said yes.'

'But how did she get the address?'

'I had given it to her during the book launch.'

'Show me the number.' I could sense a storm coming.

I dialled the number from my cell phone. 'Was her name Kajal?' I asked with panic in my voice.

'Yes, her name was Kajal.'

I opened WhatsApp but there were no messages from Kajal. She had not even wished me. Her last message was before the Kolkata launch saying, *Best wishes for the book launch.*

Lalita rubbed her palms, tension visible on her face. I regretted not telling Kajal about Lalita. Why had she come for the launch suddenly? Had someone told her about me and Lalita?'

I was mumbling all this in my head when Lalita asked, 'Who is Kajal?'

I took in a long breath. 'She was my wife.'

20

Kajal's name popping up on my birthday pushed me back into the memory lane.

My father was an English teacher in a private school in Indore. I was born and raised in a middle-class family and my mother was a homemaker. Life is usually filled with more theories than practical lessons if you have a teacher in the family and it was the same with us.

I was closer to my father. He had big dreams and never failed to encourage me to chase and fulfil mine. He believed that a satisfying life was better than a successful life.

The exceptional thing about papa was his out-of-the-box birthday gifts to me. On my fifth birthday, papa gifted me his old bat and ball set. My friends teased me upon seeing the size of the bat. The bat and I were almost of the same height.

On my tenth birthday, he gifted me his HMT wrist watch. It was so heavy that it seemed like a wall clock hanging around my wrist. Then, on my twelfth birthday, he gave me his transistor.

On the fifteenth birthday, he had gifted his uniquely designed playing card set. I was delighted to see the colourful cards. On my eighteenth birthday, he handed me his camera with the most profound words.

'Son, we can purchase anything with money, but when someone gifts you their belongings, they also pass on their invaluable memories and blessings. You deserve this camera. You have earned this, my dear boy. We all are memories in the end.'

I grasped that when you don't have the money, you have to rely on philosophy, else you cannot survive. The speech was so impactful that I started hating new things. But now, I was old enough to understand that everything cannot be dealt with in a philosophical manner. When I was mature enough, I understood how beautifully he had managed his material concerns with his ideals and beliefs.

During my school days, I loved participating in essay writing competitions and dramatics. I was an expert in comedy roles, and was mostly into writing plays. After the twelfth standard, I asked papa what I should do. He again enlightened me with a long speech.

'When making a career decision, you should listen to your intuition and feelings, but be sure not to confuse the two. Intuition is an ongoing feeling that there's something wrong; for example, over some time, you may develop the feeling that you don't quite fit into your organization. Dig deeper and try to find the reasons for feeling this way. Whatever the case may be, your gut is telling you to do something about it, so you should listen to your instincts rather than irrational feelings.'

I yawned twice, trying to comprehend it entirely. I itched my head and made the most innocent face.

'So, which stream I should take?'

'You are good in English.' This was more of a statement than a solution, but I nodded, understanding his unspoken advice.

I joined the bachelor's course in English at DAVV University in Indore. Even in college, I never had many friends. Vishal was the only one sticking around, since the beginning. We studied together until high school. Vishal and I always used to hang out at eating joints in Indore. We often went to Chappan Dukan and Sarafa market to eat jalebis. I still remember his love for poha jalebi, which was a dish the mostly eaten during breakfast and as refreshment in the evenings.

Post my graduation, I wasn't sure what I wanted to do. My father asked me the same thing. I took a few minutes and itched my head, so he announced the verdict.

'Join English M.A.'

I wondered whether he had helped me decode the career puzzle, or declared his decision.

Indore had recently developed its own IT park and a whole lot of companies had mushroomed. I had a good command over English and a college classmate had joined HGS Tech. He had referred me for the job too. I consulted papa, as always. He asked me whether I really wanted to do this. When I did not react or express any particular emotion either for or against it, he asked me to go ahead and join the BPO.

On my first day to work, he blessed me with his words of wisdom, 'A satisfied life is better than a successful life.'

Night shifts were mandatory at this company, so I enrolled for the Master's degree through the open school. That way, I could manage both, my job and education. On the flip side, it made my life clockwork. When I got my first salary, I purchased a Philips radio for my father and a saree for my mother. I reminisced how he had gifted his favourite radio to me on my birthday, and I had accepted it.

Papa's eyes held back subtle tears after opening the gift. He hugged me and tuned into a radio station where Kishor Kumar's song was playing. As the melodious voice filled the room, none of us spoke. The silence whispered how much he liked the song and the singer. He patted my back and finally said, 'After all, an artist never dies. Each one of us has to die someday, but an artist remains immortal through his work.'

Unknowingly, he had given me hope and a seemingly unattainable dream. I was good at writing plays. So, instinctively I applied my brain, believing that I have the potential to create good art and made a decision.

'Papa, I want to be an author.' I guess my heart had finally spoken, because my mind was still blank.

He smiled and said, 'An artist lives forever, but he hardly earns.'

I rubbed my sweaty palms together and took in a deep breath. I wondered whether he was supporting my dream or warning against it.

After I finished my Master's in English, I got an offer from Convergys in Pune. I grabbed the chance with both hands as it meant growth. I knew it'd be hard because the lip-smacking food joints of Indore were going to be left behind.

My father was content as he considered Pune to be the safest city in India. He had told me numerous negative things about Mumbai and Delhi, but never for Pune.

Kajal was a part of the hiring team at Convergys. She was the one who had recruited me. When I landed in the office, I was shocked to find that she did not remember me at all. I was one of the thousand sheep that she had hired. She was an arduous lady, busy with her work.

She had appeared to be beautiful, intelligent and sweet. I was immediately attracted to the vibrant city and its fashionable girls. In the office, people were so obsessed with speaking in English that sometimes it was hard to believe they lived in India.

I started to smoke at that point, twice or thrice during work hours. Kajal's office was close to the exit gate. I often heard her shouting. As abrupt as it may sound, I started liking her, for no reason. Of course, there were other pretty faces, but she somehow felt special to me.

One evening, when the weather was good and there was a lot of work piled up, I rushed outside for my need of nicotine. I noticed someone at the tea stall. I looked at the attractive HR manager and the urge to smoke doubled up. Kajal was fuming with every puff and yelling over a call, 'Why does everyone join a call centre and leave in two months? They should at least stick around for six months.'

She disconnected the call and looked at me with a question mark.

'Yes, I agree. People should stay here for at least six months,' I babbled almost immediately.

'Yes!' she said looking at me with a blank face. 'I am Kajal,' she said offering her hand, which I took immediately.

'I am Arun, and I know you pretty well. You are the one who hired me.'

'Oh! So how long have you been here?'

'Only two months,' I said, suppressing a smile, 'but surely will stick around for the next two years.'

'In call centres, no one gives a guarantee for more than a year.'

I smiled like an idiot. I could have committed my entire life at her bidding.

'Which account do you manage, by the way?' she asked.

'City Bank.'

'Hmm. Are you from Pune?'

'No, I am from Indore.'

'Are you serious? I am also from Indore.' Her gorgeous lips curled up into a smile.

I had never believed in miracles, but for the first time I felt that if you believe in something, the entire world conspires to help you to achieve it. I was pumped up with a strange energy. I loved Indore for food and now the city was no less than Las Vegas for me.

It was my longest smoking break ever. We discussed Indore's eating joints, the schools, gardens and cleanliness. She finished her cigarette and I almost jumped to pay the bill. Three more guys were eyeing me, the feeling of envy was evident on their faces. Victory danced on my face as my smile said it all. I noticed that my heart was also fluttering with excitement. I was flying, finding it tough to settle my feet on the ground. I gave fifty rupees and signalled at the man behind the counter to settle the bill for both of us. She did not say anything. When he started giving back the change, I had no mood to collect it. I wanted to say, 'You can keep the change' when suddenly Kajal blurted, 'Why did you pay my bill, bro?'

'Bro?'

My happiness died a natural death. I looked at the tea stall owner and he understood my pain and offered two complimentary candies, perhaps as a compensation for my great loss of opportunity.

I picked the cash and counted every penny I had invested on this girl. I kept the change in my pocket and hopelessness in my heart before leaving.

The next day, she came near my cubicle. 'Please ping me whenever you go for a smoke.'

'Sure. But I don't have your number,' I said.

'What is your number?' she asked in reply.

She sent me a text message as soon as I gave her my number. WhatsApp was not that popular those days.

I looked at her phone and she saved my number as "Office Arun Indore". I was just in-between office and Indore. I started hating the office and Indore was the only common thread for us. I decided to avoid her because it wasn't going to go anywhere, but how can a man avoid a beautiful girl.

When I was about to go for a smoke, I typed a message, *Are you free for a smoke?* and wondered whether to send it or not.

Sachin, who sat next to me saw me standing with the phone in my hand and said, 'Hey, don't go near her or else she will make you her bro.'

It seemed she had bro-zoned quite a few. I extended my sympathy, but I dare not admit that she had already done that to me. I was submerged in the pool of undesirable humiliation when I received a message from Kajal.

Free for a smoke?

My mind howled, 'Deny her request.' But my fingers typed, *Sure.*

She enquired taking her first puff, 'When you are going to Indore next?'

From that point, our interactions happened around my trip to Indore. There was always some parcel or snacks that were requested during my return. Her family always gave big bundles of delicacies to be carried. Basically, I was like a one-sided lover who doubled as a courier boy too.

She never called me for any other reasons. The attraction died in my heart, but the heart had to beat anyway. I remember it was Diwali and trains and buses were jam-packed. I had booked my bus ticket well in advance. She, on the other hand, tried to book the bus ticket, but everything was sold out.

Just two days before Diwali, I got her message, *Will you join me in a taxi till Indore?*

I looked at my bus ticket and remembered how much I had invested in it. A rare moment in my life, on the one hand – my phone displaying Kajal's invitation which was full of possibilities and adventures. And, on the other hand, the mundane bus ticket that promised a boring ride. Anybody could have guessed what I'd choose.

We were sitting on the back seat of an air-conditioned Tata Indica. Two relaxed souls sitting through the twelve hours of travel. There was love in the air. The driver played some breezy love songs, making the air even more romantic.

'What do you wish to become in life?' she asked suddenly.

'I want to become an author,' I replied promptly.

'Wow! Like Chetan Bhagat?'

I nodded.

She started counting the advantages of being an author – Work from home, book tours, fan following, interesting life, film rights and many more. In the end, she added 'big money'. I kept listening to her all the way. When we reached Indore, Kajal said, 'Total taxi fare is six thousand rupees, but you can pay me two thousand only.'

I looked at her and she understood that I was not in a mood to pay. So she said, 'It's okay bro!'

If I were a gas cylinder, I could have exploded. I reached into my wallet and paid her the exact half – three thousand rupees. Stepping out of the car, I snapped, 'Stop calling me bro.'

'Why?'

'Because I like you.'

Suddenly everything went silent and I left.

After Diwali, I returned to Pune alone. I still had the other bus ticket, after all. She had tried calling me before starting back for Pune, but I hadn't taken the call. In the office, I had changed my cigarette timings and changed the shop as well.

It was the third day after my return from Indore and I was busy working at my desk. I noticed someone standing behind me.

The most charming face was there to meet me and she asked with authority, 'Why are you avoiding me?'

Sachin was staring as if he had seen a woman for the first time. 'Can we go for a smoke?'

'Sure.' I stood up.

While fuming away the cigarette and her anger, she asked, 'Why do you have a problem when I call you bro?'

I did not answer. She finished her smoke and before leaving said silently, 'You are right. I should stop calling you bro... because I think I kind of like you too.'

That day, she did not object to my paying the entire bill. Just like that, we gradually started meeting each other regularly and eventually fell in love. Later, she quit smoking and joined me as a tea partner instead. Two years later, we graduated to life partners. One year after our marriage, she switched to work at IBM Daksh.

In all this time, I started writing a love story. I got a publishing offer from a leading name in the industry and I could not believe my luck.

My first book was thus published after years of hard work. I had incorporated many scenes and incidents from my own love story. The book went on to become a huge sensation. It sold close to ten thousand copies in the first six months itself. My Facebook and Instagram pages were flooded with appreciation. I invested a great deal on the marketing front to promote the book. In fact, once when I had shared my address with a few readers for them to send me their books, I was overwhelmed to see how so many unknown readers sent me gifts on my birthday. A few had expressed their emotions through love, hugs and kisses.

Success does not come alone, it brings along confidence, security, a sense of well-being and the ability to contribute at a greater level. I was on a writing spree and had written two books in a year. I was ready for the third one already.

While the appreciation for my stories was always high, the sales were constantly low. It took constant push and investment to keep things going. Kajal and I often argued about the credit card bills. The financial pressures and appreciation were increasing, but sales had slowed down, creating a sort of gap which seemed difficult to bridge.

Amidst all this, I shared my idea of leaving the job to focus on writing full time. I was of the opinion that if I gave it more time, I could push the sales quite a bit.

On the proposition, Kajal opened an A4 sheet and wrote income on one side, and expenses on the other. All the credit card bills were on her tips and royalty was on mine. She assumed the deduction of book travel expenses and free books to bloggers, and finally landed on the earning value. She wrote a ton of numbers within a few minutes like she was the finance minister of India or something. In the end, she had circled a figure of three lakh in a year.

It was the most unbalanced sheet in my life.

She prodded, 'I have not included the assumption that reading habits are going down because of Netflix and smartphones.'

The income from the books put together was not even half of what I was drawing at that time and she passed the verdict that leaving the job was a horrible idea.

Like I had done with my father for all my career decisions, I had no choice but to accept her word in this case. But on the flip side, I was smart enough to play around. I had almost stopped working in the office and after three official warnings, the organization gave up on me. I was asked to leave the company. Whether she approved of it or not, I was now a full-time author.

When I got the official email informing the termination of my contract, I was petrified. I knew too well that reality would change from that day onwards.

I booked a ticket to Indore and went to meet my family. Kajal was not too happy with the sudden decision. When I told her about the job situation, she smiled and said, 'I know you need your father.'

When I stepped inside my home, I found my father and mother smiling. One look at them told me how blessed I was to have them in my life.

'I came to celebrate my birthday with you.' I said, hugging my father.

'I am glad you came, but this decision could make your wife upset,' he said slightly worried, but I smiled.

We had a quiet dinner, just soaking in the company. Once we were done, papa asked me to join him for a walk. Sluggishly, we walked out and across the street, crossed two tea stalls and a jalebi shop. Papa asked, 'What happened? Why are you upset?'

'No, I am not upset.'

'Why are you upset?' he repeated.

'How did you know?'

'You missed your favourite jalebi joint.'

I shrugged like I'd been caught red-handed. 'Papa, I was fired from my job.'

'That's nothing to worry about. Companies do that sometimes. You will get a new one soon.'

'I don't want to take up another job.'

'Hmm. What have you thought?'

'I will write full time.'

'How much will you earn from that?'

I rubbed my eyes, took a long breath and whispered, 'Close to half of the current salary.'

'Why is becoming an author so important to you?'

'I think I want to live like an artist.'

'Every child is an artist. The problem is in figuring out how to remain an artist once you grow up.'

'I guess, I want to die like an artist then.' I managed a weak smile.

'An artist never dies.'

We laughed loudly at that

'What do you suggest, papa? What shall I do now?'

'For now, let's celebrate your birthday tomorrow!'

We went out for dinner the next day. As I held the knife, about to slice it through the glossy cake, I missed my favourite smiling face. I whispered sorry to Kajal in my mind and cut the cake.

I wondered why papa had not gifted me anything this time. Once we were home, I saw my father fidgeting with his favourite photo frame. Mom went to sleep around 11 p.m., after which I joined papa on the sofa.

'Where is my birthday gift, papa?'

He pointed at the big golden frame. The frame had held a smiling picture of papa for a long time. I went closer and picked it up, bewildered to see my picture in it. It felt like I was replacing my father.

'You know, this frame, with my picture in it, was given to me by my father when I was upset with my life; so dissatisfied and lost that I was thinking of ending my life. My father had said that according to him, I was the strongest person, asking me to keep this portrait in my room. He had also advised that the day I find the strongest person in the family, other than me, I should replace my picture with theirs.'

'But papa, *dadaji* was a freedom fighter. You have also struggled a lot. I am unworthy.'

'You are also a fighter.'

'But I am not that strong.'

'A man who decides to follow his passion and settles for half the money he is already making, don't you think he is a strong person?'

I looked at him and a tear rolled down to settle on my smiling lips. The best moments in life always bring tears and smiles, together. I looked at the smiling boy in the frame and a voice inside me said, 'I will never surrender'.

I returned to Pune with a renewed sense of inspiration, and the big frame. While things seemed to be settling, not all was smooth between me and Kajal. The differences that had earlier been hidden behind our smiles, now started surfacing. We eventually noticed that we were two very different people. She wanted to go to luxury hotels for dinner and I was gratified by eating at a dhaba. She wanted to shop in malls and I was glad to explore the Shaniwar Wada market. She loved clicking fancy pictures on her latest phone and I was still struggling with a basic Nokia handset.

Whenever she entered the house, she used to start yelling, 'Why is the room so dirty?', 'Why is the kitchen so messy?'

I am sure it was messier earlier, but I guess she wanted me to work around the house too. Or maybe, she was struggling hard to accept the fact that I was sitting at home without any corporate stress.

It was around Christmas time. She had proposed a lavish travel to Turkey. We made the budgetary calculation and the expense sheet said we would end up spending one-and-a-half lakhs. A shiver ran through me upon seeing the figure on paper. The actual expense could have been more too.

I denied, only to hear, 'You sit at home doing nothing, while I work so hard. I deserve a break.'

I went silent. I let out the breath I had been holding. My gaze lowered at the cruel onslaught. I said nothing, but my facial expressions spoke volumes, I am sure. She said sorry quickly, but it was a little too late for that.

She used to have a crazy schedule those days. She had not read any of my works, so she never had much to say on it. Once, when I was travelling for book promotion events, she was idling away her time at home and decided to read the latest book.

When I returned home, she did not hug me, nor did she ask about the book launch. She did not ask how the crowd at the event was. On the contrary, she asked, 'Do you always write about your real experiences or you imagine some too?'

I did not understand the sarcasm. She opened one of my books and said, "There is an intimate scene in this book."

'Yes, I have written that.'

'How can you write something about us for everyone to read?'

'What?'

'The moment you explained so vividly... that was our personal moment.'

'But I have changed the characters' names.'

'Have you even sold off your soul to write?'

I gritted my teeth at the crazy presumption, but didn't answer.

'You can earn nothing from writing such passionate scenes. But moving forth, I am sure it is enough to have five books in your name.'

'I can leave anything, but I cannot give up on writing.'

'What did you say? You can leave anything?'

I nodded.

She rubbed her eyes with her right palm and rested her hand on her hip. She took a step back and stood there, holding out my book in one hand. 'What if you need to choose between me and writing?'

I had never anticipated such a turn of events. Everything went in slow motion and I gazed at the golden photo frame in which I was smiling. I went closer to her and took the book from her hand and went to the other room.

She stood there stupefied, like everything had frozen for her.

The next morning was quiet like a mortuary. The dead remains of previous night's conversation were still hanging high in the air. I had a book signing session in Mumbai, so I left in a hurry, promising to speak to Kajal in the evening.

When I returned, everything had changed. Half of the almirah was empty and the washing machine was missing. The fridge had vanished, and there was a dust rectangle in place of the new smart TV. Only the king size sofa adorned the living room.

Had there been a robbery at home? I tried calling Kajal, but her phone was switched off.

My eyes landed on the golden photo frame. A neon pink sticky note was fluttering over my face n the photograph.

The day you decide to not be an author, I would love to live with you. I had married a family man, not a self-absorbed and impractical dreamer.

21

'Can I go out for shopping?' Lalita asked, holding a small cotton bag.

'What do you want to buy? Can I help?'

She hesitated a bit. I knew I was being intrusive, so I altered the question. 'Do you have sufficient cash?' I asked.

She nodded. I explained the way to the closest market complex and gave her a fancy jute bag. She did not know that plastic bags were banned in Pune. I was rattling off instructions, when her smile gave away that I must be appearing silly.

She left and I was alone in my own house after so many days. I thought of cleaning up the house, putting some papers in their designated files and organizing the bookshelf. But, all that planning in my mind was paused when I heard a knock at the door. I assumed Lalita must have forgotten something and opened the door.

In place of Lalita, I was confronted with awkwardness in the air. My expression was never unwelcoming in the past with any guest. But who was I kidding! She was not a guest. She was wearing a cream-coloured salwar kameez and her hair was tied down in a neat braid. She had lost weight from the last time I had seen her. Subtle signs of age were peeking through, but nothing strong enough to take away the beauty. Her face was radiating a magnificent glow.

I was not able to notice her properly when she came for the book launch, but now I took my time. A lot had changed from the last time we had met.

'How are you, author saab?' she said bringing me back to reality.

'Hi, Kajal!'

'Won't you welcome me inside the house?'

'Please come inside!' I said awkwardly, realising that we were still standing at the door.

She took a stroll in the hall, scanned the house, then looked at the familiar sofa in the living area and sat on it. I realized the forthcoming danger and went to the washroom to made a quick call.

'Listen carefully, Lalita! Please don't come home until I call you.'

'Okay sir,' she said almost immediately.

'Can you please repeat what I just said?'

'Please do not come home until I call you.'

'Good.'

I disconnected the call and walked out of the washroom. Kajal was exploring the top shelf of the open almirah in my bedroom. The entire top rack was filled with clothes we had recently bought for Lalita. I understood that today was going to be a tough day.

'Would you like some tea, Kajal?'

'Sure. Why not! It's been a while that I had your special tea.'

She looked at the clean and organized kitchen. I kept the kettle on the flame while she stood at the back.

'How is your latest book doing?'

'Good!'

'You have become a great author.'

The sarcasm and bitterness in her voice stung me hard. 'Why? What made you think that?'

'Huge fan following on Instagram, so many birthday wishes and positive reviews everywhere and, you have even hired a full-time manager.'

I smiled at the thought that she was snooping on me. She knew everything that was going on in my life.

'Tea is ready. Shall I serve it in the balcony?'

She nodded in response and followed me. 'Nice view and ambience here. The flat is perfect just because of this balcony space, I feel.'

'Thanks.'

She took the first sip of the tea and I braced myself. Every compliment was a signal that a volcano was now ready to explode. I accurately remembered how much we had loved spending time on this balcony and watching the view.

'So, your manager stays with you?'

It had taken her twenty minutes to get to the real purpose of her visit. There was a slight quake in her voice.

'How do you know?'

'I saw her leaving the flat. I knocked at the door after she left.'

'You are making assumptions, and all wrong,' I said.

'You have no idea what I am thinking, author saab. Where did you meet her?'

'Kolkata.'

'Bengali beauty!' she almost hissed.

'You are taking it all wrong, Kajal.'

'Okay! Then make me understand what is right.'

I finished my tea and noticed that she had not taken a single sip after the first one. She was holding the cup with both her hands, her gaze was firm.

'She is just a friend.'

'Earlier you said she is a manager, now she is your friend too?'

'She is a friendly manager.'

'Friendly manager?' She laughed. 'Are you sure?'

I nodded.

'Silence is the evidence of sin. You wrote this line, remember?'

'What do you want, Kajal?'

'Divorce!'

'Oh! So you need a divorce?'

'I will meet a lawyer next week and file a divorce petition. You can come to the same advocate and we can mutually sign the documents.'

'You did not think of that for years? What happened so suddenly?'

'That is my problem, not yours.'

'There can be nothing personal here.'

She held her chin and pouted. 'Listen, author saab, you are a respectable person in the society of fools. I know you don't make much money, but you have earned respect from many. That is more precious for you than anything else. Don't lose this respect!'

'But...'

She kept the teacup on the balcony rack and shouted, 'There is nothing left between us. Choose a new life, and a new wife.'

22

In Kajal's words

Hi, I am Kajal and I thought I should share my own story. I cannot trust Arun to do so rightfully. He has made our personal life public in the past, so I insisted on writing this.

I was born in a well-off family in Indore. Growing up, we had everything in my family. My parents never checked the price tags of things before buying them. Every summer, we would go to beautiful holiday spots. I was still in school when we had already been to Europe, Japan and Dubai.

I guess it was at the Dubai airport where I – a teenager sitting with her mom and dad, waiting to board the flight for home – saw the colourful map of the entire world. It was showing the connectivity of Emirates airlines to the world, but I scanned the entire map. Ever since, I have dreamt of visiting the entire world.

My mother was a little conservative about savings, but my father was the decision-maker. And the decision was always in my favour. The fancy clothes and branded shoes were like a need for me.

Arun and I used to bond during the smoke breaks at work initially. Ten of my hired resources had left the company within three months of joining. I was fuming in frustration on that particular day when he came from nowhere and started sympathizing. I liked him instantly.

I thought he would behave like other guys, who would try to find a reason to roam around me. But he was different. When I got to know that he was from my city Indore, unknowingly he had given me one more reason to like him. I would confess that I knew he hated my calling him bro.

I started teasing him with that word, with the hope that he would express his feelings to me someday.

Arun was studious, but crazy about stories. He was often busy reading romantic novels. I had no interest in reading, but I was always open to hearing his unrealistic stories.

Finally, one day, he expressed his feelings. 'Please stop calling me bro. I like you.'

I was a bit taken aback with his sudden confession, but things began in a new way from that day onwards.

We got married after two years of courtship. But we were poles apart. He never spent money on luxury or entertainment. A dinner date was the rarest of rare things for us. He did not even like to have an occasional drink. He never paid attention to the brands he was wearing. I rarely saw him wearing watches. His favourite dish was dal-rice or at max *panipuri*. He was more middle class than I had ever thought him to be.

When he wrote his first book, I was so proud of him. I loved this talented side of him. It made me see that he was passionate about something. His first book had taken the literary world by storm and everyone started praising him. I read the book and loved the way he had expressed the characters' emotions. It was a matter of great pride for me to see my husband being praised for being so mature and sensitive. Every day he got messages from his fans by the tons.

Soon, he had written four more books and become quite popular. I was shocked at how his female fan base had increased multi-fold within two years. He was deeply engrossed in replying on Facebook and Instagram most of the time.

One day he expressed his disinterest in continuing with his job, quoting impractical dialogues like, 'I want a satisfying life more than a successful life.'

I could understand the emotions. After all, he was well respected by many, but respect does not run homes. I explained the financial implications of this idea.

One fateful evening when I came back from the office, he told me that he had been fired from the job. He was sad and went to see his parents the next day. When he returned, he had a golden frame with his picture in it. I wondered why his father had gifted him an old frame, but it looked like Arun valued it more than just a gift.

He told me he didn't want to search for a new job and would pursue writing full-time. I had nothing left in me to argue. I accepted his unrealistic dream.

Due to the stress post his decision, I started smoking a lot in the office and stopped visiting Indore completely. It had been three years of our marriage and we did not have any child yet. At that point, I had intentionally increased my smoking. Plus, I did not want to get pregnant.

He was on his ride of mini stardom and sat comfortably at home most of the time, enjoying life. I felt jealous that I was clocking ten hours at work each day. To add to it, he started getting emails, messages and letters from his fans, especially females. He had never posted about his marital status on his social media profile pages. He said that it would help him increase his fan base.

It was heart-breaking to see that my husband's individuality was overpowered by the author in him. It kept hurting me that he never posted anything related to me or even hinted at the fact that he was married.

On our third marriage anniversary, I wanted to plan a holiday in Turkey. He did some stupid calculations and simply denied. I understood that he had no issues with an average middle-class life, which I was still struggling to accept. I had dreams, which were dying under the weight of his aspirations and ignorance.

Whenever we talked, he would start off about books and promotions. He was in Delhi for a book tour and I was alone at home. I read one of his books while he was away. I was appalled that he had written an intimate scene, taken straight out of our personal life. I could not hold back anymore. How could he put everything from our life so openly?

I read that scene again and again, not being able to come to terms with it.

When he got back, I confronted him. He didn't see anything wrong in it. It was my stupidity to give him an option between me and his writing. He made the obvious choice and I felt humiliated like never before. I was up the whole night, sitting alone. I concluded that I was an obstruction on his road to success. I couldn't help but appreciate internally that he was standing up for something he had wanted to do his whole life. It was time for me to set him free. I thought my absence would give him a moral push to write and earn more.

The next day, he went to Mumbai for a book signing event. I packed all the luxury and expensive things from the house and moved to my friend's place. I wanted to make him believe that I was a money-minded lady. I wanted him to hate me so that he could move on and become more successful, even if meant that he had to pull me down.

I gave my friend some fake story about our house being renovated. I stayed there for a month. I did not receive any phone call or even a single message from Arun in that entire time. He could have scolded me, or just sent an angry message. I saw him being active on Instagram and Facebook, like nothing had changed for him. Then, one night, I saw him live on Instagram. He was smiling and greeting everyone. I watched the live recorded video for more than ten times. That's when I decided to move on and search for another house to shift into.

23

That evening, my car had broken down. The mechanic had told me that the car needed a new spark plug and the replacement was going to be expensive. I needed to arrange some cash. I did not inform Lalita about Kajal's surprise visit. We had dinner as usual and I went out for a long walk.

When I came back close to an hour later, I noticed that Lalita was dressed very differently. Could it be that I had not noticed her before? She was wrapped tightly in a thin red gown which ended at her thighs. I wondered when she had bought that.

The gown seemed to be a bit fashionable, its sheer material falling tightly enough over her body to emphasize all her assets. I noticed something had changed on her face too. Perhaps it had something to do with her hair. She had made a small top knot, with a few strands of hair falling on her almost bare shoulders. I sat on my bed and she immediately switched off the lights. Now, the room was dimly lit with a lone bulb which radiated a red glow. Under the red gleam, Lalita appeared like a bottle of wine – exotic, rich and reddish.

She neared me and asked, 'Do you want some sweet dish?'

'What do you have?'

'*Mishti dahi.*'

'No, thanks. I am good,'

She started preparing her bed on the sofa.

'When did you buy this dress?' I asked settling under my quilt.

'Do you like it?'

'It looks nice.'

She lay on the sofa and enquired, 'What happened? You look tired.'

'I have a headache.'

'Let me give you a massage.' Before I could resist, she was already on my bed.

She touched my head and started pressing it gently. I felt relaxed. I did try to deny, but she was already on the task. She started touching the corners of my forehead and I closed my eyes.

The intensity of the massage and her touch felt a little different. She touched my back and inserted her fingers inside my collar. I opened my eyes and her bare fair thigh was right there. I turned my head to the other side. I was almost resting in between her legs, so I closed my eyes.

Goosebumps ran through my body along with her hands. She ran her soft fingers through my shoulders and around the chest area. Suddenly, she pressed my nipple and I sensed a warm breath very close to me. I opened my eyes, only to see that she was about to kiss me.

I almost threw her out of my bed. I flared my nostrils and shouted, 'Could you please go to your sofa?'

'Do you have some sexual problem?' she asked.

'That is none of your business, please.'

'Why are you not accepting your feelings?'

'Feelings?'

'Yes, the world can see it and everyone knows. I am also ready.'

'But I am not ready.'

'Do you love me?'

'No.'

'Then why are you helping me so much?'

'That is my problem.'

'But it's related to me.'

'I wanted to write a story on your life.'

She stood still, frozen where she was, whispering lightly, 'Are you a human being or just a businessman?'

'If I was a businessman, I'd make the worst of the lot. Only I know how much I am losing here.'

That night, I understood that I couldn't keep her with me for a very long time. The rumour mills were running random news, drowning my image like smoke. My social media friends and relatives had a different understanding of me now. I never thought I would be a case study for so many people. I called Vishal, wanting to meet him. He called me to the Mumbai-Pune old highway.

We were standing outside the Indira College near the famous Yewale tea stall. Vishal signalled the tea seller. The tea vendor understood the signal and came with two cups of tea. I offered him a twenty rupee note, but he said, 'I cannot take money from staff.'

'Staff? Which staff?'

He pointed at Vishal. 'Police staff.'

Vishal beamed like he was getting a Nobel Prize for his contribution in the police administration. His uniform offered us free tea. I noticed again how there was a thin line between respect and fear.

'What happened, author saab? You look worried,' Vishal asked sipping his tea.

'Bhai, I cannot keep her with me beyond this point.'

'Why? What happened?'

'Kajal got to know everything about her.'

'So Kajal is the problem?'

'No no! Actually, Kajal thinks I am having an affair with Lalita.'

'Everyone thinks that.' He quipped.

I took a sip, closed my lips and remained silent for a few seconds.

'Why don't you go to the women rehabilitation centre in Pune? Try to admit her there and get rid of all the problems?'

'But you said these places are horrible.'

'Listen, it's better to go for a bad option for her, than to stay in the worst situation you are currently in.'

I nodded. 'Let me think about that.'

He moved towards his bike and advised, 'You are thinking too much.'

'I am just trying to help her.'

'Do you have feelings for that girl?'

'Yes.'

'What kind of feelings?'

'I don't know.'

He rolled his eyes and shook his head in disbelief.

24

I was standing outside the Pune *Sarkari Nari Sudhar Kendra*. The board was written in Marathi. Vishal had shared the address over WhatsApp after our meeting. The big metallic black gate made it look like an entrance to some jail. I scanned the bigger gate and found a small movable gate. I knocked and a man and a woman dressed in security guard uniforms opened the door.

The male guard peeped out and asked, 'Whom to meet?'

'I wish to talk to someone who takes care of this place.'

'It's a ladies hostel,' he said in an arrogant Haryanvi accent.

I was a little impressed with the security thing. 'It is important to meet the manager, please help.'

'What is the purpose?'

'I wish to donate some amount.'

He looked at me from top to bottom. Maybe, my below-average dressing sense was not supporting the narrative of me being a philanthropist. He opened the door anyway.

'You can go to the office towards your right, but before that, please put your name in the register.'

I entered the details in eight different columns and the man guided me towards the office. The area was big and a few vehicles were parked in one corner. The unruly grass and shrubs indicated that the garden had been neglected for a long time.

The office I entered had three racks of files on the table with many almirahs, one printing machine, one computer and about six wooden chairs. A layer of dirt on the computer keyboard indicated how much it was used. I looked up and noticed a CCTV camera. I assumed it was faulty.

A lady came shouting on the phone. She gaped at me, the unwanted visitor, but I remained seated at my place. I was confident because I knew one police department official who would come to save me in any case. It's good to have a close friend who works in the police.

I made a mental note of a series of questions that I would have to tackle.

She finished the call and took her seat, '*Kaizala? Kon ahes*?' she asked in Marathi.

'Actually, I wish to admit a lady here, and before admission, I wished to know about the place.'

'Who is this lady? How do you know her?'

'She is just a random deprived lady.'

'Where was she before?'

'Actually, she was working in a red right area.'

'Prostitute?'

'It takes nothing to respect someone.' I stopped blinking my eyes and said with a stiff face, 'Call her a lady please?'

'Sorry sir,' she said with a cunning smile on her face. 'Of course, we can admit her.'

The smile on her face confused me. 'Can I see her picture?' she asked like I was a close friend.

'Why do you want to see her picture?'

'Just curious to see her.'

I tried to read between the lines.

'I don't have any picture.' I said in a cold voice.

'Sir, please leave the premises. Men are not allowed, and we only take admission via the police.'

She stood up from her seat and again started shouting at someone in Marathi. In between, she kept glaring at me. My questions were still unanswered. I stood up and started walking towards the exit. The female guard was passing a winning smile.

'What happened saab? You look upset,' the male guard sympathized with me. The disappointment was visible on my face. But I thought of giving it one last try.

'Can you tell me any tea joint nearby?'

He pointed at the tea corner just opposite to the building. 'They serve delicious *vada pav*. I had one yesterday.'

The drooling words indicated that he was hungry. I wondered if he was actually hungry, or was it just the *gutkha* in his mouth.

'Would you like to have a vada pav with me?'

'No sir, I am fine.' His eyes and smile were saying something else.

'Arey, please join me. I would love to pay.'

He spit all the gutkha and gulped a sip of water before walking with me towards the joint. We ordered two vada pavs and tea.

'Where are you from?' I enquired

'Panipat, Haryana.'

'Nice. How long have you been working here?'

He did not answer. The joint owner served the food and tea in the meantime. It was a plate of huge sweet bun with masala potato inside, with tangy chutney to go with it.

'How long have you been working here?' I asked again.

Before he could talk, he stuffed his mouth with vada pav. I understood that there was no point in talking to him right now.

When he had finished, he said, 'Two years. I have been working here for two years now.' The achievement of the association was evident on his face.

'Is this place safe?'

'I eat here daily. There is no problem with vada pav here.'

'I was talking about the Nari Sudhar place, not vada pav.'

'Yeah, it is absolutely safe.' He smiled and winked at me.

'But I have heard some hidden stories around the women's hostel, especially at night.' I winked back.

He narrowed his eyes and passed a look like a roadside pimp luring his secret customer. 'You are wrong, sir.'

'Oh! Means no funny business, right?'

'You can have all the fun in the day because night out is not allowed.'

'What does that mean?'

'You choose the place and take her with you in the day. Just make sure she is back before evening.'

'Oh!' I made a face. 'Are all women from the hostel involved in this?'

'Not all, but which one do you want?' I was stupefied. Suddenly the lady guard signalled at him.

'Sir, I need to go. I cannot leave the gate unattended for a long time.'

'Wait, take one plate vada pav for her as well.'

He collected the parcel in a few seconds and whispered, 'Don't you worry sir, this place is safe.'

'Yes, this place is safe, but the women are not.'

I came back home, discovering the harsh realities of life. I had never been more convinced of the pain and suffering that seemed to be made for women only. I stepped into my small perfect room and looked at the well-organized bed, the golden frame on the wall and the smile on Lalita's face. I noticed how blessed I was.

I settled on the sofa and a spicy aroma floated in the air. It was an indication that dinner was being made. I typed a long message to Vishal, requesting him to find another centre for Lalita.

I sat on the sofa, closed my eyes, kept the phone aside and took a deep breath.

'How was your day?' Lalita asked.

'It was good, thanks. How was yours?'

She smiled and went back into the kitchen. I checked my Instagram and people had flooded it with quotes and memes. I replied to a few messages and put the phone aside. It rang unexpectedly, though with a known number. I pouted, looking at the caller's name and then answered,

'Hello Kajal!'

'Where are you, Arun?'

'I am at my home, why?'

'Could you please open the door?'

'Why? Where are you?'

'I'm outside.'

Her call brewed tension in my head. I looked at Lalita and concluded I should not hide her. I opened the door. Kajal was standing there with a cold smile. This was our third encounter and second interaction in the last ten odd days.

I opened the door and welcomed her inside. The last time she had walked, her face showed a sense of sadness which was concealed by her smile. Now she was standing there, exuding authority. She stood tall in jeans and kurta, her arms folded. The makeup was missing from her face. I understood that the bad day was still on.

Kajal was staring at Lalita.

'Do you want something to drink?' Lalita asked politely.

Kajal did not display the slightest courtesy. She did not even offer usual greetings.

'You did not introduce her,' Kajal said to me, completely ignoring Lalita.

'She is my manager.'

'What is she managing?'

'My work, my social media...'

'So she is managing all your needs?'

I withheld any words that came to my mind as an instant response as I did not want to utter anything stupid.

'Why don't you try your hands at writing erotic books? I guess you can write it well now.' The sarcasm in the statement and taunt in her voice was evident.

'Can we talk outside?' I asked motioning towards the balcony.

'Who is she?' she questioned me, the moment we were in the open space.

'Listen, Kajal! I don't think this is the right time to talk. You look distraught.'

'I need an answer.'

'Please ask a straight question then.'

'What is your relationship with her?'

'Why are you even interested in her?'

'I have nothing to do with you and your personal life. But I cannot accept that someone like her is staying with you.'

'What do you mean by 'someone like her'?'

'You are going around with a prostitute!'

'Stop it!' I screamed. 'Please don't call her that!'

'Then what should I call her?'

'She is a lady.' She nodded as I asked her, 'Who told you about her past?'

'That is not important.'

I went silent to avoid any unnecessary discussion. She waited for a few seconds before saying, 'Get rid of this girl right now, or else I will post on Facebook and Instagram that you are…'

'Why do you hate her so much? Just because of her past? Which is not even her fault.'

'I cannot accept that someone like her is replacing me,' she screamed right back.

'If you spend just one night with one of them and talk to them about their life, family and circumstances, you'll find that she's just like any other woman.'

'Seems like you have spent many nights with her.'

'Please don't insult her.'

'You are fighting with me for such a girl?'

'Any woman who sells her body is infinitely less of a sinner than many who insults her for no reason.'

'I was insulting you, Arun. Not her.'

25

Kajal left and there was a deadly silence in the room. Lalita and I both stood facing each other. I behaved as if nothing had happened.

We had our dinner in silence, and I tried to ask Lalita a few questions just to lighten the atmosphere of gloom. She just answered them in one word or simple nods. We prepared to go to sleep right after dinner. I was thankful that this day was finally ending. I was sure I couldn't handle any more shocks.

I turned off all the lights, except for the night lamp. I lay on my bed, staring at the ceiling which was bathed in red light, waiting for a peaceful sleep to take me into her arms. The tricky part about sleep is that the more we want it, the more it evades you. While tranquility was nowhere to be found, anxiety was trickling through my mind. I thought about how Lalita and I had met. I even questioned myself as to why I felt so connected to her. Was I doing something wrong?

I got up and noticed that Lalita was sitting.

'What happened Lalita?'

'Nothing sir, I am just missing my friend.'

'Oh, which friend?'

'An old friend.'

'Okay.'

'Sir, could you please help me?'

I nodded. 'I have a relative in Asansol. Could you please book a ticket for me to Asansol?'

'A relative? You never told me about any relative before this.'

'No actually, we...'

I cut her short with my raised voice, 'Where was this relative when you were struggling in Kolkata?'

'He didn't have a job back then, but now he is better off.'

'Shut this nonsense, Lalita!'

'Why?'

'You are not going anywhere.'

'Why are you suffering so much for me, sir?'

'That is my problem. You leave it to me.'

She nodded and I could see tears gleaming in her big eyes. I clenched my fist and looked at the floor.

'Why do people hate us?' she broke down like a little girl.

I had no answer and walked up to her.

'Why sir?' This time she looked straight at me.

'You had two options – life or dignity. You chose life.'

'Is there something wrong with what I did?'

'Ask anyone who has been in your position. They might have walked on the same road.'

'But people do not accept us.'

'We are all social animals. Perhaps more animal than social.'

Her expression changed and she smiled, and then laughed like a fool.

I did not know how much she had understood. 'I guess it's late. We should go back to sleep.'

She went and switched off the night bulb too. There was absolute darkness in the room.

I slept soon after, but when I woke up in the middle of the night, I saw some light in the room. Lalita was doing something on her mobile. I left my bed secretly. It was pitch dark and she did not notice my presence. I peeped into her phone. She was checking her mom's picture. Then, she started looking at a series of images with another girl. She was a young lady and was smiling in all of the pictures. Lalita had many pictures with her.

I cleared my throat to announce my presence, surprising Lalita and making her straighten up a little. Then I summoned my courage and asked, 'What happened? Why are you still busy on the phone?'

'Nothing sir, I was chatting with an old friend.'

'Oh, you have never told me about her.'

'Yeah, I left that place and she is still there.'

'What is she doing?'

'The same thing that I was doing.'

Somewhere, this sentence hit me. I was only looking at one Lalita and then I realized there are many other girls like her out there. I decided that whatever the ending may be, be it good or bad, someday I would capture their story in my book to ensure that their voices are heard.

'What did she say to you then?'

'Leave it, sir! You have already had enough.'

'I am sure I can hear more.'

She took in a long breath before saying, 'We used to share our dreams while we stayed in that brothel. I had a weird dream... to leave the place and become somebody's someone. She used to laugh at me, saying that I shouldn't live in a bubble. People can sympathize with us, make sad faces, and even give money, writers can write stories about us and NGOs can give excuses, but eventually, no one would accept us.'

'That is not true.'

'Till yesterday, I held that my friend was wrong.' She took a pause and her struggle to speak was noticeable. 'But today, I feel she is right.'

26

Next day after lunch, I packed an extra T-shirt, shorts and a water bottle, ready to leave. I informed Lalita that I was going to Lonavla to meet my friend.

She nodded and I wondered what she would do the entire day, all by herself. An unpleasant experience and nothing to do in life is the biggest challenge. I rubbed my hand on my forehead.

An idea struck me. 'Lalita, please get ready. We are going to Khandala.'

She smiled and went to the washroom to change. She stepped out in tight-fitting jeans and a baggy T-shirt. She had even applied a light lipstick. There was a huge smile on her face. She looked like a smart teenager. One look at her and you'd think she had never seen a wild party, she had never flirted with a boy, she had never used any expensive smartphones and she was never genuinely loved by anyone. What was her mistake?

I revved up the car and we headed towards Lonavla. She sat in the front with me and started asking a lot of questions.

'Are we going to Khandala or Lonavla?' There was enthusiasm in her voice.

'Both are close by.'

'Okay.'

'Have you ever heard about Lonavla before?' I asked Lalita.

'No, but I have heard about Khandala.'

'Oh! Have you been to Khandala?'

'No, actually from that famous Aamir khan song... *aati kya Khandala.*' She smiled.

'Is this your car?' she asked.

'Yes, I bought this car when I was still in the job, and when my wife was also earning. It was financially a good time. Things started getting worse when I left the job.'

'Hmm, do you have any plans to join the office again?'

'No dear, I have lost enough just to stand tall in writing.'

She scratched her head, unsure of what I meant by that.

The freshness in the air had indicated that we were nearing our destination. The evergreen Khandala was cool and refreshing. Lonavla was the most preferred location for a quick getaway, especially during monsoons. Amid the pitter-patter, the quiet hill station was popular for its hillocks, caves and picturesque lakes.

Lalita poked her head out of the window and started swaying her hands, feeling the chill in the air. We had crossed the monkey point. She was delighted to see the monkeys and the people gathering around, feeding them. I bought roasted corn from a roadside hawker. She grabbed a plate of corn bhajiya along with two hot cups of chai.

After a few turns, we reached the Lonavla police station.

'Are we going to the police station?'

'Are you scared of the police?'

She nodded.

We walked into the police station and a person greeted me at the gate itself, 'Namaste Arun ji!'

'Namaste,' I replied

Most of the police staff knew me around there. We sat at the corner on a large wooden chair. Lalita was exploring every corner of the police station. On one wall, Gandhiji was smiling like all was well. The second wall captured the sad looking bespectacled Dr Ambedker. The only other empty wall space was decorated with a map of Maharashtra and a giant notice board. There were few inspiring quotes written in Marathi.

The notice board displayed pictures of wanted criminals. Even though the picture quality was terrible, I noticed that how most of them looked innocent. I realized that we should not judge people by face value.

Vishal came and hugged me. Lalita offered a respectful namaste.

'Please come inside.'

He welcomed us to the private interrogation room and instructed Lalita to sit on the sofa. We were far enough for her to overhear our conversation.

'How come you are here without any notice? Hope you are not roaming around Khandala with your girlfriend?'

'Can we talk about something serious?'

'I also need to talk about something serious.'

He frowned and I said without blinking, 'Why did you tell Kajal about Lalita?'

'How did you guess?'

'Because no one else knows all that about Lalita.'

'She was calling me almost every day to check about her. And by mistake...'

'By mistake, you vomited everything?'

'Sorry yaar.'

'You have made my life harder, bhai.' I sulked.

'I know.' His reply further worsened how I felt. 'Even Kajal called me. But I have a good news.'

'Good news, really?'

'I have found a women rehabilitation centre in Mumbai.'

'Hope this one is good.'

'That is the best place for ladies like Lalita.'

'How is the education standard there?'

'Education? What are you up to?'

'Nothing. Just tell me how are the facilities for education there?'

He rolled his eyes and said, 'I don't have such specific details, you can visit the place and ask.'

'Oh, then how do you know it's a good place?'

'Stupid, I enquired for you. I am a police-wala, remember?'

'Okay, thanks. Could you please arrange for me to go inside and explore the facility?'

'Writer saab, it is a rehabilitation centre for women. Men are not allowed inside the premises.'

'But I want to see and inspect the place, Vishal.'

'Why are you doing so much for her?'

'Truth cannot be said, and I don't want to tell a lie.'

He looked at me for a few seconds and started pacing in the room. He looked at me with a cunning smile. I understood he was about to explode a bomb of an idea.

'You can use Kajal.'

'Why would she help me?'

'Because that would indirectly help her as well.'

He passed a winning smile and I reciprocated with a sly smile. Two sharp friends can explain the entire plan to each other with just an expression. We chatted for some more time on mundane things, like how Lonavla was getting polluted nowadays. He even served us the best tea and bhajia.

'Are you going to stay overnight?'

'I had originally planned to stay, but I am with Lalita... so maybe next time.'

He nodded.

'I have one more request.'

'You need some cash?'

'How do you know that?'

'When you came with Lalita, I understood everything, author saab.'

'Smart man.'

'You cannot milk the same cow every time.'

I smiled at his strange dialogue, but still went to milk my favourite cow. 'Can you lend me fifty thousand?'

'Fifty? All well? Your royalty will be coming soon. Can't you wait till then?'

'I have to buy a few things for her as well.'

'I don't have money for such nonsense.' He looked angry now.

'Don't say that, bhai.'

'You are wasting your money on her.'

'Please don't say that.' I wondered how to handle him.

He asked me suddenly, 'Can I ask you a very personal question? Just answer in a yes or no.'

I flushed, but nodded, nonetheless.

'Do you like her?'

'Yes.'

'Do you love her? Be honest.'

'Yes.'

'Do you want to marry her?'

'No!'

There was silence for a few seconds. Then, he turned his face to the other side, slowly pulled out a cigarette and lit it ignoring me. He took the first deep puff and said, 'I guess you should leave. It would be risky to drive on hilly roads at night.'

I silently left his cabin and found Lalita sitting in one corner. I signalled at her to leave.

'You look upset,' Lalita said as soon as we got inside the car.

'No. Nothing like that.'

I drove the car in silence, thinking about my friend. How he had turned his back on me. How we had grown up together and how I had funded his expenses when he was short of funds to purchase a car. How we had spent weekends on Kashid beach together.

All memories came flooding into my mind. I wore my sunglasses, not daring to show my tears to Lalita. I also increased the volume of the music player. However, my mind was hearing a different tune.

'Was I so wrong that even my best friend had refused to help me?'

I got an Instagram notification.

Congratulations! You have reached the one lakh milestone.

How ironic could life be! I had one lakh followers and friends online, yet I couldn't stop thinking about my one true friend.

We reached back home an hour later. I stepped inside the house and my eyes landed on the big golden frame. I removed the frame from the wall and kept it inside the almirah. I did not have the scope to eat anything as I felt exhausted. I switched off the light and covered my disappointment with darkness, under my quilt.

The mobile phone vibrated with a message.

Dear user, your account has been credited with 50,000 rupees.

A WhatsApp message also popped up from Vishal.

I am proud of you, my friend.

27

I went to the car service station and the service engineer looked at my car, sympathizing with the machine. 'It's been twelve years, but you are using the same Santro car. Hyundai has launched a new model of this car now, sir.'

His sympathy for the car was embarrassing for me.

I couldn't even think how much more money I would need to get the car repaired. When I returned home, Lalita was busy working in the kitchen.

I opened the cupboard to keep some bills, but the documents were not at their usual place. I pulled the drawer to open it fully and noticed that all the documents were stacked neatly. I searched for a T-shirt and it was misplaced. Everything was at a different location. The unattended socks were perfectly stocked in the lower drawer and handkerchiefs were all cleaned and ironed. A blissful feeling ran in my mind. I checked for the album which I hadn't been able to find.

'Where is my album, Lalita?'

'The wedding album?' she asked from the kitchen.

'Yes.'

She opened the almirah and I saw that the album was nicely wrapped inside a women's dupatta. I beheld the dupatta that had belonged to Kajal. It was the only belonging she had left behind. Kajal took everything, except the bundle of memories that I cherished. I unfolded her dupatta and the big collection of memories landed in my hand. I looked at Lalita and expressed my respect and gratitude for making this house a home again.

After thanking her, I said, 'You are not here to clean my house.'

'I thought this was my house too.'

Her words shook me. I pretended to be busy with the album.

She moved to the kitchen and I understood she did not want to face me. She had made the moment easier for me. I opened the album after three years. Kajal was smiling as a young and beautiful bride. A happy man was standing next to her. It was the most authentic smile I had seen on my face.

I checked the pictures of our honeymoon. We both were playing on the wet sands of the famous Phuket beach. There was an image of us at the Phi Phi island beach. It had been years since I had gone for any trip whatsoever.

I pulled out one beautiful wedding picture from the album. It was taken just after the wedding ceremony. I wrote a few lines at the back of the picture and put it inside an envelope.

'Hey, Lalita! I am going outside for a few hours.'

She nodded.

I reached Kajal's apartment after twenty-five minutes. It was my first visit to her flat in all these years.

Should I have called her before coming? Or do I have the right to visit her anytime? I could not decide.

Suddenly, the door opened. We looked at each other for a few seconds.

She was dressed in fashionable pink shorts and a soft white T-shirt with a floral print. It was an effortless fusion of an alluring and nonchalant look. It complemented her natural charm flawlessly.

'Hey Arun! How come you are here?'

'Sorry, I should have called before coming.'

'Stop behaving so nicely. Come inside!'

I walked in and found a grand luxurious sofa sitting proudly at the centre of the tastefully designed living room. The fridge was familiar to me; I was seeing it after three years. The walls were blank, however, the central wall had a big Ganesha painting screaming silently that I am very expensive.

'It's a one BHK,' she said and walked to her kitchen.

The outstanding kitchen was very well managed, just like we see in hotels.

'You live alone? I mean, do you have any roommate?'

She offered me a glass of water.

'Won't you offer me tea?'

She stretched her arms and her body language said, don't try to act smart with me, and she said out loud too, 'Seems like you have some hidden agenda.'

I smiled at the thought that she knew me so well. She opened the fridge, took out the milk and started preparing tea. I was exploring my options to start the conversation. My mind questioned, did I still have the authority to ask any favours from her?

The presentable room, a shining kitchen and the luxurious sofa revealed that she was doing fine in her job.

'How is the job going?'

'I got promoted as senior HR manager in TCS.'

'Wow! But I heard you work with some NGO as well.'

'Yes, on weekends.'

'That's great.'

'How are your books doing?'

'Nothing new. Teenagers are busy with smartphones and everyone wants a free copy.'

'But recently, you announced that you sold ten-lakh copies.'

'So you follow me on Instagram?' I passed a sly smile.

'Don't say you are still the same struggling author! You have one-lakh followers and a dedicated manager.'

I almost laughed at her sharp comments.

'I guess you are doing what you always wanted to do,' she said, handing me a cup of the freshly made tea. There was a winning smile on my face. I had come here like a loser, and now felt like I had the upper hand.

'The tea is good, thanks.'

'You are not here for tea. That is for sure.'

'Yes, I need help.'

She took in a deep breath. I had played this game with her in the past. Whenever I needed any help, I set my ground. She folded her hand in a posture which said that you cannot divert my attention. I took the first shot anyway.

'I am shifting Lalita to a women rehabilitation centre in Mumbai. Men are denied entry into the facility, so I want you to drop her and confirm certain checkpoints.'

'What checkpoints?'

'Things like the stay arrangements, educational facilities for girls and whether she'd be safe there or if women are exploited for trafficking and...'

'Why are you so worried about her education?'

'It will help her in future... to build a better life.'

'What is your relationship with her?'

'I guess you already know how I met her, Kajal.'

'I know all about that, but why are you doing so much for her?'

'That is something personal.'

'Fuck off, Arun! Tell me the truth, else...'

'If I tell you the truth, would you help me?'

'Don't try to play with me.'

I closed my eyes and looked down. 'Okay, when I met her for the first time, I presumed that all red light area girls had no moral values, no self-respect, because no dignified woman will ever sell her body. But one night, Lalita gave me a massage and when she was about to leave, I offered her some cash. She denied and said, "Sir, I don't need your sympathy".'

'What is so special about that?'

'When Lalita said she did not need my sympathy, I realized that she had not yet died internally. If she has not lost the battle, then how could I?'

Kajal picked up the teacups and moved towards the kitchen. She washed the cups while I stood behind, waiting for her to say something.

'What is your relationship with her?' she finally asked.

'She is a friend, a roommate let's say.'

'Arun, why are you trying to be a hero?'

'I am just trying to be a good human being.'

'What made you think I will help you?'

'Because you are a social worker.'

'You have so many fans and followers, including social workers. Anyone can do this. Why me?'

'But I want *you* to do this for me.'

'I cannot help you... sorry ...'

'Don't deny it, please.'

'You have no right over me.'

I understood that I had lost many things now. I got up from my seat, leaving the envelope with our wedding photo on the couch and mumbled, 'I know it will be difficult for you to sleep tonight.'

'You please don't worry about my sleep.'

28

In Kajal's words

I had loved Arun dearly. And, had been waiting for months and years in the hope that someday he would realize his mistake. I mean, passion is okay, but you cannot give up on your loved ones for it. But, I was wrong. He was so busy with his new life as a successful author that he started writing more. Now, he was releasing two books in a year. He was riding on the wave of popularity and appreciation. It was like he did not need me at all, and my going away had given him everything that he had ever wanted. I was jealous of his success, more so at not being a part of his world, and blocked him from Instagram and Facebook. But how could I stay so aloof! A few months later, I had created a new account as Naina and followed him.

One should never underestimate the power of jealousy. It had turned me into a great detective and I had even tried to chat with him on Instagram and asked about his books. He had replied earnestly to a reader, and I purchased and read his books. All of them.

I changed my job and joined TCS as a corporate HR manager. It was the biggest Indian IT company and it was a moment of pride for me. But I had no one to share the happy moment with.

In trying to find some solace for my shattered self, I joined the corporate social responsibility team and spearheaded it. Noticing my hard work and dedication, I was soon promoted as the head of the corporate NGO funding. I had found a new purpose in life, structured around development of women and their rehabilitation.

In the last one year, I had been to many NGOs and initiated several programmes to make their education facilities better.

After almost one-and-a-half years of leaving Arun, I thought of taking a divorce. Many friends had suggested the same, especially because we had not been in any kind of contact. Reconciliation looked nearly impossible in our situation. I had approached an advocate and taken his advice too.

I decided to initiate the legal divorce proceedings, but gathered from his Instagram posts that he was not in town. It was around Diwali and he had gone to meet his family in Indore. I was distraught, because here I was! Gathering the pieces of our failed relationship, not going to visit my family also. On the other hand, it did not seem to have any impact on him and his life.

On Diwali, mom called me in the evening, wishing me and enquiring about my well-being in general.

'Why did you not come home for Diwali, beta? It would have been so nice.'

'I was busy in office, mom. Couldn't make it.'

'I understand. Thanks for sending Arun, though.'

'Arun came there?'

'Yes, why?'

Arun had gone to see my family even when we were not on talking terms for more than one year. He met my family and projected that everything was fine between us. I wondered whether he had something in mind. I did not understand him.

I told mom that all was well, but till when could we lie to our dear ones? One day, mom found out that we had separated long ago.

Somehow, her finding out was the final nail in the coffin. I accepted everything and decided to move on. It had been more than three years without him now.

We both were busy in our respective lives. But, I was in regular touch with his friend, Vishal. I often contacted him for police verifications and NGO-related documentation. Arun had also become a part of the big league of authors and came out with his tenth book. I thought of making him happy on this special occasion. It had been a long time of separation and I crossed my fingers and walked into his book launch, hoping that we could both move on – even if on our separate ways.

I was stunned to know that he had a female secretary with him. I wondered how he could even afford her! Was he merely wasting his money? Or had his books really started doing that well? My curiosity compelled me to meet the girl. She could barely talk, leave aside communicate in English. The way she spoke, I understood that she was a display doll, just sitting on exhibit. The detective inside me deliberately asked about her address and I was shocked to know that she was staying with him.

I had always believed that an author lived in a crazy fantasy world with unrealistic expectations. Arun had been no different all along, and I was further saddened to see that nothing had changed about him. I made a surprise visit to his home, which now I regret. If it hadn't been for that day, I wouldn't have lost my peace. Two things broke every bit of faith inside me – one, he was the same meagre author, whom the world assumed to be a rich man; and second, Lalita was staying with him.

He was an ideal guy for his fans, especially females, but how could he settle for a woman who was close to fifteen years younger than him? I searched about that girl on Instagram, Facebook and everywhere else, but failed to find anything concrete.

And when one day I spoke to Vishal for work, he mentioned casually that someone was seeking help regarding women rehabilitation centres in and around our area. He mentioned a Bengali sex worker and I connected the dots. The girl had not been there on his Kolkata launch, and had abruptly landed at the Pune launch. She was also Bengali, so maybe it was the same girl Vishal was asking about.

I called Vishal the next day and bluffed that Arun had told me everything about the girl. Not knowing the truth, he told me everything about Arun and Lalita. My ex husband had gone beyond all limits and started sleeping with a whore! I did not shed a tear.

Anger is like an acid that can do more harm to the vessel in which it is stored. It had made me a dreadful person. But after more than three years of not showing any inclination towards me or our relationship, the impractical author walked into my house with an unusual request. There was a winning smile on his face.

How dare he! How could he ever think that I would help a girl like her? I don't know if writers are usually crazy, or he had lost his mind? Or did he have some hidden motive behind that?

He left the place, disappointed. There was no way I was going to commit to helping him.

I closed the door behind him and sat on the sofa, struggling hard to control my emotions. There was an unattended envelope on the sofa. I recollected Arun had been carrying this when he walked into the house. I opened it and took out the wedding picture. I looked happy and young and the man was smiling. My mind kept asking whether I should help him? Was it some kind of last request before we parted ways forever? I flipped the image and saw a note scribbled on the backside. A drop of tear rolled out from my eye. I read the note again,

I am not an author, I am just a husband.

29

I withdrew some cash from the ATM and went to a printing lab. I shared the picture on my mobile phone with them.

'Can you print this image for me?'

The printing lab employee took a quick look at the image and asked, 'What size and paper quality would you need?'

I explained the requirements in detail. He advised me to come after half an hour. This meant I had thirty minutes to waste and I remembered all the necessary things that I needed to buy. I bought a travel bag after checking a few in various stores. I checked for space while recollecting Lalita's belongings and concluded that the bag I had picked up was large enough to hold her stuff. Next, I went to buy some essentials and toiletries like soap, toothpaste, toothbrush, etc. Once I had all that, I went back to the printing lab. I collected the large print and returned to my flat.

When I came home, I walked straight to Lalita and gave her the bag I had bought for her.

'How does the bag look, Lalita?'

She took the bag in her hand and ran her fingers over it, 'Wow, this is quite nice. Also pretty spacious.'

I started explaining to her how one could wear the bag casually over the shoulders and other advantages. 'You can pack your stuff in this very easily. You are heading out to a new city tomorrow. It will be a new place and a new life for you.'

'Oh! Does that mean I am finally going to the right place?'

I nodded with a deep sigh. She took the bag and kept it on the same sofa that she had been sleeping on. She started packing her belongings without another word. Her expressions changed as she picked up all her belongings and started throwing them into the bag haphazardly. She was packing so frantically that it seemed she wanted to run away as quickly as possible. I was sitting on the sofa and watching her pack. Eventually, I helped her pack properly. Once we had finished keeping everything, she sat down on the sofa, exhausted.

Seeing her bag made me feel hollow, as if I'd never see her again.

'Are you going to drop me tomorrow?' she asked me.

'I'm not sure. Maybe someone else can drop you?'

'I don't want to go with Vishal,' she said with a downcast face, like a kid. I smiled.

'Tell me sir, what can I cook for you today, for the last time?'

The words 'last time' echoed in my mind. Her eyes were locked with mine. She asked me again, 'What shall we cook for dinner?'

'Let's have dinner outside. We can go to some place that you may like.'

'I don't know any place here.'

'I asked what kind of place.'

'Let's go to a place where couples go. A place where a husband goes with his wife or…' she paused, '…a boyfriend goes with a girlfriend.'

I felt a sense of empathy for her. She deserved at least this little joy as she would be gone tomorrow. I walked out into the balcony and lit my cigarette.

'Get ready! We are going out for dinner in half an hour,' I said taking a puff of my cigarette.

I looked up at the sky. Pune was dark and cold that day, the air heavier than usual. I took out my phone and searched for the best restaurants for couples near me. The search results came up with majorly advertisement links that either wanted me to take a club membership and enjoy a weekend or simply focused on the ambience of their sitting area. None of them mentioned about the food or the prices. So I logged in to another app and the site guided me through a lot of options. A few clicks later, I found the perfect choice - The Sayaji Hotel and Restaurant on the Mumbai-Pune highway. I read the estimated price for the dinner and it was about two-thousand rupees for two people.

Before I could decide anything, Lalita stood in front of me wearing a short dress. It was the same dress I had seen her in on the first day in Kolkata, the same shade of lipstick and the same high heels.

'Could you please...' I wanted to ask her to change the dress.

'How am I looking?'

'It looks great.' I was delighted to see her happy. 'Should we head out then?' I said and moved to pick the car key. But, she stood there without moving.

'Are you not going to change?' she asked looking at me from head to toe.

I looked at myself and decided that I should probably change. I went to my almirah and picked up a white shirt.

'Wear a red shirt. It will match my dress,' Lalita said.

I flushed and gave her a strange look. She appeared like an innocent girl with dreamy eyes and fantasies in her heart. I picked the only red shirt I had. When I was ready, Lalita applied some hair gel on my dying asset. She had managed to give me a new hairstyle with a few strokes of her fingers. I gazed at myself in the mirror and asked myself, 'Am I looking like a pimp?'

Once we were in the car, she took my phone and swiftly unlocked it. She did not bother asking for my permission and knew the lock pattern anyway. She clicked on a romantic song from my playlist, increased the volume and we both enjoyed the song in silence.

After forty-five minutes or so, we reached the hotel. It offered five-star accommodation with a large, outdoor pool and many dining options. It was a pioneer in organizing events and parties. Years ago, I had been there for my office weekend party. The spacious air-conditioned lobby and a comfortable seating area offered a warm welcome to its guests. The ground floor had the Torque Poolside Lounge, which excelled in delicious Asian cuisine. Inside the lounge, well-dressed couples were sitting on every table. The restaurant manager approached us. I requested a corner seat. He looked at Lalita and smiled at my request. The slow music and corner seat added peace to the ambience.

The waiter offered us the bar menu and I politely denied it, 'Just give us the dinner menu.'

'Can I order a drink?' Lalita asked quickly before the waiter could take back the menu.

'Yes sure.'

'One large Blender's Pride with soda.'

'Only one? We have happy hours.'

'Make it two,' Lalita said.

'Two large Blender's Pride?' repeated the waiter.

The complementary plate of roasted nuts and *papad* were served in no time.

'How often do you drink?' she asked.

'I don't drink.'

'Oh yes, I remember that from when we met in Kolkata for the first time,' she said as if it was years back.

The waiter came towards us and passed a small decorated paper and pen. 'Sir, you can request your favourite song for the live music players.'

'Which is your favourite song?' I asked Lalita.

She wrote something in Bengali as I looked at her, clueless.

'You don't hear any Hindi songs?'

'Pardesi pardesi jaana nahi...'

'Oh, really?'

I tried hard to recollect where I had heard that song before. The last time I had heard it was when I was travelling by train and had watched two kids singing the same song, asking for money. A weird feeling ran through my mind. She had finished one large peg by now, as if it was a glass of lemon juice. The happiness on her face had multiplied and she seemed to be swinging. She excused herself and went to the washroom. I wrote the same song from *Raja Hindustani* and signalled the waiter

'Could you please request him to play this song?'

'Are you sure sir?'

'Yes, any issue?'

He simply stood there and looked at me with a poker face. He stretched his hand and I understood what he wanted. I handed him a hundred rupee note and he beamed, 'What is ma'am's name?'

'Lalita.'

Lalita returned from the washroom and a voice echoed in the dining area. "We have a special song request and this song is dedicated to Lalita madam."

To my disappointment, he played a remix version of the song. It looked like someone had torn apart the original song and threaded it with a thousand needles that pierced into one's ears. But it also appeared that I was the only one who didn't appreciate the remix and almost everyone around the lounge joined their hands to clap. Lalita also started clapping as if she had got an Oscar. Everyone settled back after a few seconds, but Lalita was unstoppable. She continued to clap throughout the song.

Lalita finished the rest of the drink in one go. I was scared that the situation could get out of control. I picked the main course menu to order food. Lalita asked in a dramatic voice, 'Will you come to drop me to Mumbai?'

'I am not sure.'

'Will you come to meet me in Mumbai?'

'On one condition. Only if you will study well.'

'Study?' She made a face. 'Will they teach me English?'

I smiled.

'Can I ask you a question?' she hesitated. I nodded.

'Why can't you marry me? Is there something wrong with me?'

This was clearly the alcohol talking. I decided to leave the place before things went worse. So, I signalled to the waiter for the bill. Lalita, on the other hand, was comfortably settled in her seat, refusing to leave. She was unmoved but her smile and wet eyes were speaking volumes.

'I guess we should leave,' I said trying to get up from the seat.

'No no... please tell me.'

The waiter came and handed me the bill, just as Lalita asked, 'Tell me! Do you love me or not?'

The waiter passed a smile and I quickly paid the bill, rushing out of there with Lalita.

'Why can you not marry me?' she asked me for the fifth time since we got into the car.

I did not answer. What could I say!

'Why did you save me from that hell if you cannot accept me?'

'I accepted you as a friend.'

'You are a bad man,' she said, rushing out of the car.

'Lalita, please come back inside the car.' Before I could say anything else, she vomited on the pavement. I came out and helped her while she emptied out her stomach. Then, I helped her back in the car. I reclined her seat and opened the car window.

Her eyes were half-closed and she kept mumbling, 'I don't need your sympathy.'

30

On reaching home, I helped lay her down on the bed. She was in a semi-conscious state. Her clothes were riding up, displaying her thighs, and all her makeup was now smeared. I helped her out of her shoes and tucked her inside the blanket. She snuggled in and slept soon after.

She seemed to be at peace and I looked at her for a few minutes. The song *Pardesi pardesi* came to my mind and I smiled. I decided to doze off on the grand sofa for the night, but sleep was far away. I went to the balcony and puffed a cigarette, recollecting some old memories. I appreciated how my father had made me smile even when he had nothing. I went inside the room. The golden frame was still shining in the dim light and I was smiling in it. I pulled the frame towards me and opened it up from the back. I removed my picture and replaced it with Lalita's. I viewed the frame and questioned myself, Is she worth enough?

I wrapped the frame in a big plastic bag and counted some cash, stuffing it into my back pocket. I sat on the sofa and took a long breath. I was going to be discharged from my duties, but still, my eyes and mind were occupied. I went out for a walk. The freshness and calmness in the air made me feel very serene.

I had walked two full rounds around my society building when my mind was engulfed with thoughts again. Is this the right decision? Is Kajal brave enough to understand my signals? I cooked up some plans and decided to execute them the next day, wondering how it would work out eventually. Suddenly my phone vibrated and there was a notification on WhatsApp. It was from Kajal.

I will come to drop her tomorrow. Let's do it in the first half.

It was 2 a.m. already, and I understood that I had made Kajal restless too. I came back to the room and slept with a lost voice, but a victorious smile. I woke up around 9 a.m. The room was already clean and Lalita was sitting on the bed with a guilty face.

'Good morning Lalita!'

'Good morning, sir.'

'Can you make a cup of tea for me?'

This was the first time I had asked something from her authoritatively. She nodded and went to the kitchen. She served the tea on the sofa.

'So what is the plan?' she asked while I took the first sip.

'Kajal will come to drop you to Mumbai. She will be here in an hour.'

'Are you sure?' she asked, surprised.

'Yes.' I cleared my throat and continued, 'Listen, I need to tell you what to expect at the rehabilitation centre.'

She nodded silently.

'They will ask you for bank details and other ID cards.'

'I have an Aadhaar card, but I don't have a bank account.'

'I know. I will arrange that for you. They will give you a form and you need to share the family details along with other information.'

She was perplexed.

I explained all the details with a pen and paper. She heard the instructions and pleaded. 'Why can't you drop me till Mumbai?

'There is a reason.'

'What reason?'

I thought for a second and said, 'It's a women's hostel. I am not allowed inside.'

She went silent.

I had already dropped a text message to Kajal, asking her to pick up Lalita in an hour. Lalita cooked a large bowl of paneer curry and rice. I checked the quantity and realised that it would be sufficient to last me two days. I appreciated her concern for me. Also, she was cooking in my kitchen for the last time. She zipped up her bag after collecting the last bit of her belongings from my house and sat on the sofa.

'I am ready.'

'Okay! Kajal would be here soon.'

There was silence in the room and she constantly looked at me. She kept sipping water every five minutes.

'I need to give you a gift.'

'I don't need anything,' she said sternly.

I ignored her and went towards the almirah. I unfolded the big golden photo frame.

She looked at the frame and her eyes widened. I had owned the framed picture for the last five years, and now, she was replacing me. She simply stared at me and did not react.

'This is for you. My father had given me this when I was making a new beginning. He had also told me, "When you meet the bravest person in life, you should put their image inside this frame".'

She was silent and tears were flowing from her eyes.

'Whenever you feel you are weak and the circumstances seem to be taking the better of you, just look at this frame and I am sure it would help you.'

'I am not a strong girl.'

'Every girl in your situation is a brave girl. You have faced so much in life, and still haven't given up.'

She hugged the photo frame and sat on the sofa. Her sobs felt like silent cries, drowning the whole house in melancholy. I did not stop her. Sometimes it is good to cry and vent out all the emotions which are latent within you. I moved to the balcony to avoid my share of tears.

The knock at the door distracted me. I understood Kajal was here. Lalita went to the washroom to clean her face while I opened the door.

'Ready?' Kajal asked.

'No, I am not ready. Something urgent has come up and only you and Lalita will be going.'

'I thought you will be coming with us.'

'Sorry. Please come inside. I need to explain something.'

She sat on the sofa and I passed on a list of instructions.

'You need to ask about the college, the quality of education. Ask if they are allowed a night out without permission? Lastly, will they help her to get a job?'

She heard all this and shook her head in disbelief.

'And one more request.'

I pulled out the cash from my back pocket and gave ten thousand rupees to her. 'Open a bank account in her name with any bank, and share ATM and other things with her.'

She looked at the cash and her face flushed. 'Seems your books are doing great'

'I have borrowed this from Vishal.'

She flared her nostrils. Lalita was already at the door, ready to run away from the place. I offered to carry her bag, but she politely denied. We walked towards the lift, in absolute silence. Clearly, Kajal and Lalita were still avoiding any opportunity of talking to each other. I wondered how the journey from Pune to Mumbai would be for them.

Kajal ignited her car engine and Lalita quietly seated herself on the adjacent seat.

Lalita looked at me and my mind registered that I was seeing her for the last time. At the last moment, Lalita opened the car door and hugged me. She was drowning me and herself in a pool of tears. Kajal was watching us with a strange expression. Lalita continued to hug me for a few minutes and said, 'Thank you... Thank you, sir.'

She had never shown her gratitude to me before. I understood she was treating me like a stranger now. I stood there like a rock, not showing a single emotion. Lalita sat inside the car with a forlorn face and Kajal waved me a formal goodbye.

I went to Kajal's side and said, 'Be brave to take tough decisions.'

She frowned and put the car in first gear. The car started moving away with my love and my wife. My two favourite people had left. I stood there for a few minutes before returning to the room. I switched off all the lights and lay down on the bed. I closed my eyes and cried for a few minutes, fervently praying after what seemed like ages. 'God, please help my Kajal take the tough decision.'

31

In Kajal's words

It was a rare moment. Two ladies were travelling together and yet it was completely silent inside the car. I wondered why Arun did not join us. Was something cooking in his mind? Did he love this girl so much that he couldn't bear to watch her leave? I had become a great detective in real life. Lalita was continuously looking outside the car. Being the senior one, I thought I needed to break the ice.

'Hi Lalita, should we introduce each other?' She nodded.

'I am Arun's almost ex-wife, Kajal.' I offered my right hand for a casual handshake.

'Hi, I am Lalita, his fake ex-secretary.'

We both laughed. Two broken people always make for great company.

'Tell me something about yourself, Lalita.'

'Feel free to ask anything, ma'am.'

'Call me Kajal, not ma'am.'

'I call him sir, so it is obvious you will be ma'am.'

'Okay, whatever you deem fit.'

I could sense some turbulence in her voice. It seemed that she was battling an internal war.

'So, you have never been to college?'

'No. Just basic schooling.'

'Why did you not join college?'

'The college was far from my village.'

'Did you ever hope that you will leave the red light area one day and settle down in life?'

'I stopped thinking about the future long ago.'

Her words were sharp and straight. It was hard to imagine what she must have gone through. I crossed the mesmerizing Lonavla. I had gone through these lanes many times in the past.

'Let's have a quick snack?' I offered and she nodded.

I parked the vehicle and ordered two teas and two Irani bun maskas from a nearby restaurant.

The cool breeze was refreshing. The lush green area was like a blessing. I got up from the table and came out to explore the serene weather. Lalita too followed me. I tried hard to interact with her, but she lacked manners. We finished the short break and left the crossway. The car stereo had not been working for the last two days. The deadly silence was so uncomfortable, and Lalita was making it all the more worse.

'Can I ask you something?'

She nodded.

'Why does he love you so much?'

'He never loved me. He only cares for me.'

'Concern is another way of loving someone.'

'No, it is not. He is simply a good man.'

'Do you have feelings for him?'

'No.'

I frowned and resumed my focus on driving.

'Can I ask a silly question, ma'am?'

'Yes.'

'Why do you still love him?'

'There is nothing between us. We have walked far away from each other and are on different lanes now.'

'But I guess there is a lot between you both.'

'Whatever made you think so? Did he say anything to you?'

'I know many things. I was his secretary, remember?'

I went silent. I did not like her implication.

'For the last three years, he never came to meet me and the only time he came was for you. So it is clear that he...' I did not complete the sentence.

'You know how many followers he has on Facebook? Instagram?' Lalita asked.

'Around one lakh on Instagram and two lakhs on Facebook,' I said, almost gritting my teeth.

'And he gets an average of twenty messages daily, from new readers.'

'So what?'

'Why did he pick you?'

'I don't know.'

'Maybe because true emotions do not need to be flaunted. They are sincere and subtle.'

I did not like her words, but they had some grain of truth which was hard to ignore.

'You know why he never pursued you after you went away? Because he did not want you to struggle with him in a lower middle class lifestyle,' she said.

I went blank and pretended to pay attention on the road. A part of me was feeling proud of this man.

'Can I ask a personal question?' Lalita asked.

I nodded and appreciated internally that she had some manners, to confirm before asking personal things.

'Can you give me a single reason as to why you guys separated?'

I thought for a few minutes. 'Because we were fighting a lot.'

'Why were you both fighting?'

I recollected my old memories, and it was hard to think and answer in a simple line. I could not say it in one line or one reason.

'You did not answer me?'

'Because we are different?'

'So how do you see us? Are we the same?'

'What does "us" mean?'

'Arun and Lalita. Is there any similarity? We never fought.'

'So you have now started calling yourself "us"?'

She laughed. She laughed like an idiot. I wanted to throw her out of the car.

'Why are you laughing?'

'Nothing... sorry.'

'Tell me what was so funny.'

'It's funny how you both love each other so much and have still been living separately for so long.'

32

In Lalita's words

When Arun sir gifted me the big golden photo frame, I was taken aback. But the message was clear. Today was my last day with him and I may not see him again. I was trying hard to control my emotions. When I looked at him, I could see that his eyes were moist too. There was an inexplicable vibe floating in his eyes. He tried to avoid eye contact.

I was a little surprised to learn that Kajal would be taking me to the rehabilitation centre. He guided me on how to fill the forms and what formalities I would need to fulfil when I reached. I understood that Mr Author was not a person who could surrender easily. He was trying to fix as many things as possible at one go. He was working hard to get his wife, whom I guess he still loved very much, and he was also trying to look out for me at the same time.

I understood that I did not belong, and this was not the right place for me. I kept my luggage in Kajal's car. When Kajal started the engine, I looked at Arun sir for the last time. The entire month's journey flashed in front of my eyes. How he had helped me escape from Kolkata and how he had fought for me with his best friend.

He had done so much for me in just one month. Others had been with me for years, and yet, they could never look beyond their vested interests. He was the only good thing that happened to me, and I wanted to be close to him for the last time before the final departure. I came out of the car and hugged him, not caring two hoots about Kajal.

I sat back in the car and noticed how upset Kajal looked. We did not talk. Both of us tried to avoid each other. I was busy looking at the beautiful landscape, but Kajal broke the silent wall between us after a while. I realised why she was helping her estranged husband, even though she hated me. I understood one thing about both the husband and wife – they both loved each other. I decided that I had to play my part so that it could all end well.

We had some cold conversations. I guess she did not like how I articulated my thoughts as the conversation ended up being short. Somewhere I got a strange audacity and I tried to question her about her relationship with Arun sir. I laughed when she started getting jealous of me. I realized that we both were losers in our respective battle.

We had crossed the beautiful Lonavla. She drove us to a bank and helped me open an account and she even deposited ten thousand rupees in my account.

'Who paid for my account?' I asked Kajal, curious about where the money had come from.

'Can you believe that an author did that?'

We both laughed. She looked good when she laughed. It felt as if I had found a temporary friend in Kajal.

Arun sir's action had clearly shown my place in his life. I was an unspoken duty for him. Kajal and I had some heartfelt conversations about life and other aspects, taking us both by surprise as to how much we could relate to each other.

Finally, we entered Mumbai. It was all people and traffic everywhere. It reminded me of Kolkata. I had a bad feeling about Mumbai. After a five-hour drive from Pune, finally Kajal parked the vehicle outside Mata Kasturba Naari Sudhar Grah. We walked in and Kajal said something to me that echoed for a long time.

'You are about to begin a new journey. Our paths may be different, but we all have the same destination.'

33

In Kajal's words

I assisted her in opening a bank account. When I was submitting the cash, I wondered how much Arun loved her to loan such a large amount. I questioned myself as to what I was doing there. Why did he want me to help her open the account? Why did he not come to do such silly things? Was he that busy?

As soon as Lalita's bank account was opened successfully, I dropped a message to Arun and he immediately replied with a '*Thanks*'.

In the late afternoon, we had reached the centre. It had a big gate at the entrance, but the interior was not that huge. At the gate, there was a male and a female guard. I showed my Rotary Club ID card and made an entry in the visiting register before we both walked in.

Inside the compound, there was a garden that was nicely maintained. It had a few marigold flowers. The cleanliness around said that this was one of the few well-maintained centres. Half of the area was open and the rest was occupied with a four-storey building. I scanned the building and could see girls staring at us from the various windows of the building. There were no balconies, it seemed; just windows. Inside the main building, the wall was decorated with great quotes. I stopped by a quote by Mahatma Gandhi.

A man is but a product of his thoughts. What he thinks he becomes.

We walked to the reception area. It was a decent-sized hall. The walls there were adorned with images of Rani Lakshmibai, Sarojini Naidu and Bhikaji Cama. A sense of pride ran through me on looking at all those women freedom fighters. The one line I read more than ten times while sitting at the reception was:

Hate the sin, not the sinner.

I don't know why this line hit me so hard. A lady in her forties appeared after a few minutes. I introduced myself and gave my social work foundation identity card.

'Please sit, madam,' she extended courtesy.

'Thank you.'

'Lonavla police already called me and informed about your arrival,' she said, handing me back my card.

'Thanks.'

'Is she the lady?' she asked, pointing at Lalita.

'Yes. Her name is Lalita.'

'Welcome, Lalita,' she said with a smile.

Lalita returned the smile.

'I have some queries and concerns. Hope you don't mind answering?' I asked.

'Please feel free to ask.'

'Where do you send these girls for education? I mean, which colleges or schools?'

'We have tie-ups with the two universities – one is Smt Nathibai Damodar Thackery Women's University and second is Maharashtra University. Both provide good education and fees are also exempted.'

'What about books, uniform and other expenses?'

'Since we deal with mature girls, they take up jobs and earn.'

'If they will be working, then when will they study?'

'We are helpless on that account, madam,' she said and shrugged.

'Are men allowed inside the premises?'

'No males are allowed beyond this point.'

'Are women allowed to carry mobile phones?'

'Yes.'

'What is the curfew time?'

'They have to return to the centre by 9 p.m. or they have to take advance permission by mentioning a clear reason.'

'How is the room condition?'

'Her room is ready. So if you want, you can also stay here tonight. In fact, Inspector Vishal told me that you might stay here for the night.'

'Oh no! I will be leaving in an hour.' She nodded as I updated her.

'There is a small formality. You need to fill this form. Do you know how to write?' She asked while handing Lalita the form.

'Yes, I know Hindi and Bengali,' Lalita said.

'You can fill the details in Hindi.'

'Can I see the room before filling the form?' The detective in me was constantly warning me.

'Sure.' She called out to a staff member, and minutes later, a woman came into the room.

'Could you please show them the room?' The staff nodded and guided us to the first floor and opened a door. This room would be Lalita's next home.

The room was around the size of my bathroom back home. Half of the room was filled with bags of groceries, grains and cotton clothes. It looked like they were using it as a storeroom. There was a big window, but no balcony. I had never seen such a huge window.

'Wow, nice window!' I said.

'Madam ji, this was a balcony, but they have converted it into a window,' the caretaker said.

Thanks to the big window, at least the room was an airy one. Lalita and I sat on the bed.

The lady guided us towards the almirah. 'You can use half of the portion, as other roommates use the rest of it.'

'So, two people stay in this room?'

'Three, actually. But because of the grocery and the grains, we can only accommodate two for now.'

I always had my own room and suddenly I felt that I had been so lucky in my life. The caretaker helped to stack Lalita's luggage in the almirah, except for a big package that Lalita held on to strongly.

When both of us stared at her questioningly, she spoke softly, 'It's a photo frame and I would like to hang it on the wall.'

The lady left the place and now only we were left alone in the small airy room.

'Whose photo are you carrying?'

She unravelled the plastic around the golden frame and handed it to me. I looked at the frame. I had seen that frame before.

'Arun sir gave me this.'

'Do you know what that frame meant to him?' I asked realizing that it was the same frame that his father had given to him.

She shrugged like a kid who was happy with a helium balloon. I remembered that the frame was given to him by his father when he had decided to become a full-time author. I scanned the photograph of a smiling Lalita almost ten times. It appeared that a brave girl was fighting an unknown battle, and I could see Arun's love for her. I was flooded with respect for them, and I started feeling so small.

'What happened?' Lalita asked.

'Nothing,' I replied.

'Sorry if that frame offended you. Arun sir changed the picture.'

'No no, it's okay. But why did you show it to me? You could have opened it after I left.'

Her hesitation spoke more than her words. 'Arun sir had asked me to show you this. Maybe he wanted to make you feel jealous.'

He wanted me to see the frame. He had planned something. Was he trying to say something? I looked at that frame for a few seconds. I took out my mobile and texted Arun.

The rehabilitation centre was good. I have dropped Lalita in the hostel and would return back in a few hours.

I got his reply almost immediately.

Every important decision comes with some regret. Be brave to make a decision.

I did not understand what he was trying to say, but there was surely something which I needed to know. I needed to leave as it was already getting late and I was not comfortable driving at night. I pulled two thousand rupees from my purse and handed it to Lalita, but she refused.

'I don't need this money. Let me start a new life. I have already taken so much from you both.'

I wondered whether she was being an idiot or just dignified. But her refusal to take this easy money also brought in a lot of respect for her. I felt like I was the only practical person stuck in the middle of these two impractical people. I wanted to shout at her, force her to take it, but I did not have the authority to do so.

'Let us go to the reception and sign those forms.' She nodded in understanding.

I was sitting silently and scanning the quotes in the reception area, while Lalita was filling the form.

'I have completed it,' Lalita said after completing the form and handing it over.

'You need to sign here in the form as you have come to admit her,' the lady said, extending the form to me.

'Sure.'

She guided me to the places where I needed to sign and I looked at Lalita's zig-zag writing. It looked like a class fifth student had written it. I wanted to read through the document before signing it. It had the usual details such as her name, permanent address, mother's name and father's name. I looked at the father's name section over and over. I was glued to it. I had seen this name many times before. I read it again.

'This is wrong information. Why have you mentioned Arun's name in the father section?'

She was stupefied and the hostel warden said, 'Don't worry, let me strike that and correct the name.'

Lalita blocked her hand before she could cut the name.

I wanted to question as to why she had mentioned his name as the father. She looked at me and her eyes had tears when she said, 'He asked me to write his name in there.'

I recollected the series of events and opened my mobile phone to read Arun's message again with a new understanding.

Every important decision comes with some regret. Be brave to make a decision.

He wants this decision to be taken by me. I looked at her and I struggled to speak, but we both understood. After gathering the courage, I asked, 'Will you be my daughter?'

'No! Today you will sympathize with me, but tomorrow, I will be a burden on you.'

'A daughter can never be a burden,' I pleaded

'No.' Her tears were almost choking her.

I stretched my arms and said, 'Can I hug my daughter?'

She resisted at first, but later we hugged and she kept on saying, 'I love you, mom'.

34

I had been sitting inside for a long time and went out for some fresh air. I walked till the nearest store and purchased a fresh packet of cigarettes. Once home, I switched on the television and spent some time flipping through the channels, not deciding which one to stop at. My body demanded some food and I headed towards the kitchen. I took out the curry that Lalita had prepared and two bowls of rice. I walked into the drawing-room and noticed I was alone. I looked at the wall and my photo frame was also missing. I realized that many things seemed to be missing from my life. I had my lunch in silence. After a while, my mobile buzzed with Kajal's message.

The centre was good. I have dropped Lalita in the hostel and would return back in a few hours.

I replied to her message with what I had said to her in the morning.

Every important decision comes with some regret. Be brave to make a decision.

I went to the balcony, having lost my appetite and lighted a cigarette and then two. It was just a matter of time that I had consumed an entire pack. I came to the room and a series of thoughts struck me. Why am I an author? What was I getting out of it? Why did my father fool me? I lay on the sofa and tried to sleep.

I tossed and turned, changing my pose every couple of minutes. It was already 9 p.m. I had wasted three hours just tossing on the sofa.

Suddenly someone knocked at the door.

'Are you there?' It was Kajal's voice that came from the other side of the door.

'Yes, Kajal,' I replied, getting off the sofa in one swift motion.

I opened the door and found Kajal standing there with Lalita. A smile flashed on my face on its own. Lalita looked the same, but Kajal was angry. There was a sense of confusion on her face. She walked in without permission and asked, 'How many cigarettes have you smoked?' It had been years since she had asked me that question.

'Sorry!' I said.

'I need some clarification. Can we talk alone?'

I looked at my room and thought the balcony was the only area where we could sit and talk. Lalita settled on the sofa.

'Why did you do that to me?'

I stood there stupefied.

'Could you please speak up?'

I shook my head.

'You plotted everything, didn't you? You deliberately assigned the task of dropping her to me. You left our wedding photo on my sofa. You changed that framed picture and you wanted her to show me that. You also asked her to write your name in the father's section.'

'Yes!'

'Why did you play with my emotions? Why make me take that call? Why are you so afraid to make a tough decision?'

I remained silent. I tried to talk, really did, but everything got stuck in my throat.

'It's your decision and you need to be bold enough to stand up for it.'

I nodded like a scholarly student.

'Please take care of your daughter. I am leaving now.'

She collected her bag and walked away.

'Wait...Kajal!'

She turned to face me.

'I am tired of living alone and I thought I could stay with my daughter and her mother.'

'So you want a mother of a grown child?'

I had both, a smile and tears. 'No, Kajal. I want a daughter, a wife, and most importantly... I need a family.'

She closed her eyes, tears now running over her cheeks.

'It took you three years to say this?'

I went close to her and hugged her, mumbling, 'I missed you dear.'

Epilogue

We adopted Lalita legally and shifted to a bigger flat. Lonavla police helped us with the adoption papers. Lalita was busy taking lessons, and loved the English and personality development classes. She was excessively occupied with studies. She often made faces before going to these classes, but Kajal was a strict mom and she often pushed hard for Lalita to study.

Once Lalita asked, 'Why do you guys force me to study?' And she got a lengthy scolding from Kajal. I sat there and enjoyed watching the mother and daughter argue

'Dad, this is too much!' Yes, she had started calling me dad.

I avoided intervening between the mom and the daughter. My long-term peace was more important than the short-term combats.

Lalita and I took charge of the dinner. I loved cooking and had plenty of time to do that too. Kajal was still busy hiring people in TCS.

Lalita and I often smiled seeing Kajal's struggle in a corporate job. My Twitter and Facebook replies were taken care of by Lalita and every day she posted something cute and motivational. I only took care of Instagram.

One day, as I stood in the balcony of our new home, missing the exceptional view I enjoyed in my previous flat, Lalita questioned me, 'Why do you always have time and mom is always busy?'

'Because I am an author,' I said laughing.

'One personal question?' I nodded, giving her permission.

'All authors post their pictures about trips to international locations and dinners at five-star hotels or showing off their prosperity in Dubai mall or something. But you never post such pictures. Why?'

'I can barely manage to go to five-star hotels for dinner, let alone foreign trips. I am happy in my simple and humble ways,' I said smiling at her.

'But, we should make a plan to go somewhere '

'Where do you want to go?'

'Any big city will do.'

Sadness ran through my mind and I felt helpless. I looked outside and noticed that there was renovation underway in our society. There was a huge heap of sand down there. I looked at that and a weird thought made me smile.

'How about Dubai?'

'Yes.'

'Okay, then let us go to Dubai.'

Lalita was surprised as we went downstairs. Lalita queried as to where we were going. I took her near the sand heap I had seen from my balcony and asked Lalita to stand near me. I took a selfie by only keeping the sand in the background and posted the same on Instagram with a caption:

Guess the country...

Almost immediately, I got two replies. One saying Saudi, and another saying Bahrain. Then came almost ten comments saying Dubai.

I replied to one of the Dubai comments, *Correct guess.*

Lalita flushed, 'This is not fair.'

Suddenly Kajal replied on the same post.

If father and daughter have finished their Dubai trip, then please come home. We need to go to Lonavla.

I flared my nostrils and concluded that a wife is the best detective.

In the evening, we went to Lonavla. It was crowded as hell and jam-packed, but still green and refreshing. I walked into the Lonavla police station. Lalita was not comfortable visiting a police station even now, so I went inside alone.

Vishal was getting transferred to Aurangabad and probably it was the last time that I would get to meet him in Lonavla. Vishal was still with criminals and managing heaps of files in the police station. We hugged each other and he ordered a cup of kadak tea. We were busy recollecting some of the old memories when one of the junior police constables walked in dragging a lady.

'Please sit there!' The constable said in a harsh voice.

She was wearing a red short dress. The lady was shivering and sweating. She was continuously looking at the floor. Fear and regret were visible on her face. I asked Vishal what she was there for, and he whispered, 'Sex racket!'

Something jolted me as I watched her. I walked up to her and offered her some water. She took a few sips and thanked me.

'What is your name?' I asked.

'She is a prostitute,' the constable said in a harsh tone.

Vishal neared him and hollered, 'Always call a prostitute a lady; you have no idea what she has been through.'

hello! all my reader friends!

If you want to know

some crazy things about me,

scan this QR code.

I am sure you will be thrilled.

Or log on to

https://srishti.pub/rapidfirewithajay